Recommended by *Library Journal* and *Booklist*

It promises to be the most exciting year in Jean Chelton's young life. A high school senior, Jean for the first time has a steady boyfriend. And even though her parents and older brother disapprove, even though her school work suffers, Jean can't help overflowing with the confidence and happiness that come with loving someone and being loved in return.

But love is a gift fraught with hazards, as Jean finds out when brought up short not only by the growing intensity of her and Andy's feelings, but by the shock of learning that a classmate has had to leave school because of pregnancy.

Forced to re-examine her own attitudes, Jean finds no easy answers to her problems, but does achieve a more mature outlook that promises well for the future.

* * *

"Written with understanding, honesty, and good taste."
—*Booklist*

IT COULD HAPPEN TO ANYONE

Margaret Maze Craig

A BERKLEY HIGHLAND BOOK
PUBLISHED BY
BERKLEY PUBLISHING CORPORATION

SBN 425-01812-1

BERKLEY HIGHLAND BOOKS are published by
Berkley Publishing Corporation
200 Madison Avenue
New York, N.Y. 10016

BERKLEY HIGHLAND BOOKS ® TM 758,135

Printed in the United States of America

BERKLEY HIGHLAND EDITION, MARCH, 1970
2nd Printing, August, 1970
3rd Printing, February, 1971
4th Printing, April, 1971
5th Printing, September, 1971
6th Printing, April, 1972
7th Printing, June, 1972

JULY

CHAPTER ONE

The Friday night Y-Teen dance was almost over when Jean Chelton saw Andy Decker. He was standing in the archway leading from the reception hall to the gym, and he was alone. Georgia Kane wasn't with him.

Virginia Montrie, with whom she had been dancing, said in a low voice, "There's Andy."

"I know."

"He's all by himself."

"So I see."

"You ought to speak to him."

"Speak to him?" Jean echoed. She saw that Andy was scanning the crowd. Looking for Georgia, probably. "How can I? You know darned well that he and Georgia Kane are going steady."

"What difference does that make? Georgia isn't here, and even if she were, there's no law that says you have to be a clam. I should think, after what he said to Barney—"

"But that was ages ago. And it didn't change one single thing." She'd hoped, for a day or two, that what he'd told Barney might mean something. Barney had told Lynne, Lynne had told Katie, Katie had told Virginia, and Virginia had lost no time getting on the phone to relay the information. Andy Decker thought she was cute.

He might just as well never have said it. Nothing, certainly, had come of it. It had been a chance remark, made a month ago, and forgotten immediately by its maker.

"Even so," Virginia said. "You could—" She stopped, and excitement came into her voice. "Jean, he's looking right at us. Why don't you—no, you won't have to. He's coming over."

"No, he isn't," Jean said. "He couldn't be. He probably wants to check records, or—Virginia! Where are you going?"

Virginia was backing away. "I'd almost forgotten. I

5

promised Susy I'd meet her in the snack bar."

"You can't!" Jean said. "Not now! Virginia, you just can't!"

But Virginia could. Virginia was already halfway across the gym, Virginia was nodding to Andy as she passed him, Virginia was gone.

And Andy Decker was standing before her. *Andy Decker.* Why did she think him so special? There was nothing about him, not really, to set him apart, unless it was his height, or his extreme thinness. He had straight dark hair, cropped close, and eyes that were an odd green-brown, and there were freckles on the backs of his hands. He wasn't handsome. Lots of the girls didn't even think him good-looking. Yet, for months, the mere saying of his name had been a verbal talisman. Now, though, she seemed bereft of the amulet, for she couldn't say his name, she could only manage a soft "hi."

"Hi, Jean. Having fun?"

"Yes."

"Not much of a crowd. Guess it's too hot."

"Typical July weather." She hoped her smile was more effective than her words. "I feel absolutely limp." She was. Her blouse, so fresh just a few hours ago, was sticking to her back, and though she never wore stockings, and seldom socks, in the summer, the calves of her legs felt damp. As for her hair—

She started to push it back, but stopped as Andy said, "Let me." Lightly, very lightly, his fingers brushed across her cheek. Deep within, she felt a tremor. It was almost a shiver, except that it couldn't have been, not in ninety degree weather.

He smiled at her. "I'd ask you to dance, but I can't seem to get enthusiastic about anything but a tall, cool drink. I was thinking that maybe you might like one, too. How about it? Want to run out to Miller's?"

Jean's thoughts spun. She was only beginning to assimilate the fact that she was even *talking* with this boy. And now he'd suggested *Miller's*, the drive-in restaurant so popular with dating couples! Why, it was exactly what she'd been dreaming ever since late spring, when, near the close of her junior year, what the kids called the "statistic" of Andy Decker had suddenly hit her. But an

6

invitation just didn't happen this way! Not on a hot summer night, not at a Y-Teen dance! She was asleep. She was in her own home, at 123 Harriott Avenue. She was lying in her bed, and in a moment she would wake up, and Andy Decker would be across town somewhere, but he wasn't, he was right here in the gym; and so was she. And he *had* asked her. He was waiting for a reply, and already his smile was fading.

"I'd love to," she said. "But—" She stopped. She'd almost blurted her uppermost thought. *But what about Georgia?*

"But you came with someone else. Right?"

"No, I didn't. That is yes, I did, but it was Virginia, and she's spending the night with Susy, so that's all right, but I think I'd better tell them, and if you don't mind waiting a minute, I'll be right back, because I'd like a tall cool drink, too, and thank you."

"Whoa! Some place in that torrent of words there's got to be an answer. Was it yes or no?"

Be calm, she thought. And cool. And collected. "It was yes."

"And there was something about Virginia? And, I think, Susy?"

"Yes, I've got to tell them."

"Good. I'll meet you by the door, then, in five minutes." He hesitated. "I can count on it?"

She nodded, and he strode away, his hands in his pockets, his step almost bouncing. She watched him briefly. His walk, she thought, is like him. It's—well, it's just Andy. She turned, then. She couldn't stand here, watching. She'd have to find the girls. Wouldn't Virginia be surprised?

Virginia wasn't surprised. She wasn't even impressed. "I figured you'd be going home with him," she said rather coolly. Virginia never gushed. She never wasted words. She was, Jean sometimes thought, so precise that she would insist on an oral dotting of the "i's" and a crossing of the "t's," if it were possible to do so in conversation. She had a way of ignoring trivia and coming to the crux of a question that was at times helpful, at others disconcerting. It was disconcerting now when she added, "I wonder where Georgia is."

7

Jean was troubled. "So do I. I would hate to have her think—but I don't believe Andy would—maybe they've broken up."

"You hope," Virginia said. Then she relented. "I hope, too, Jean. Call me tomorrow."

"I will. First thing."

Jean wished, as she hurried up the stairs from the snack bar, that she had time to comb her hair and do a new lipstick job. But she couldn't afford to chance it. Andy might get tired of waiting, he might have changed his mind, he might have—

He was by the door, as he'd promised. He said, "*There* you are," and his smile was exactly right for the words.

Mr. and Mrs. Darwin, the Teen-Inn advisors, looked up from their desk, smiling too. But then they looked from Jean to Andy and back again. As though they couldn't believe what they were seeing. Nor were they the only ones. Liz Perkins and Marge Grubholz and Leroy Arnst, who were deep in conversation at the window, broke off and stared.

Jean knew what they were thinking. She knew what they'd be saying, the minute she and Andy were gone. "Hey, did you see what I saw? Not Andy Decker and Jean Chelton, surely?" And then the inevitable: "But what about Georgia?"

Well, what *about* Georgia? She couldn't ask Andy, could she? Anyway, there was nothing wrong in just riding out to Miller's with him, was there? Why did people have to get so excited? It wasn't as though she were double-crossing a friend. She didn't even particularly like Georgia.

With a swift reversal of feeling, she thought: But I do like Andy. And there's something called principle. I guess, deep in my heart, I know I shouldn't be doing this. I wouldn't, if it were Freddy, or even Leroy Arnst. But I can't seem to help myself.

Andy seemed unaware of her inner conflict. "My bucket of bolts," he said, "is around the corner. And I'd better warn you. I always check with a girl on her accident insurance before I let her ride with me. I don't know from one day to the next what's going to fall off or cease to

8

operate. I'm haunted by broken tail pipes, or missing piston rings, or—"

She forgot about Georgia. "Or a dead battery, or points that need checking, or a fuel pump that has to be replaced?"

Andy grinned delightedly. "Well, what do you know? A girl who speaks my language! Where did you ever learn so much?"

"I've got a brother."

"That explains it. Say, you're not Bill Chelton's sister, are you? The Bill who graduated three years ago?"

"The same. Why? Do you know Bill?"

"Not personally. But I know of him, naturally. He got a Carnegie, didn't he, for pulling that kid out of the river a couple of years ago?"

"Yes."

"I understand that he's a darned nice guy."

"Bill's a sweetheart."

"My respect for him increases. Any guy whose kid sister would speak of him with that kind of enthusiasm has got to be all right."

"How do you know so much about the way kid sisters speak about big brothers? Have you got any?"

"No. I'm Mrs. Decker's one and only. But I've been around, child. Behind these old eyes lie pictures."

"Oh, sure. And back of those old ear drums are—"

"Don't say it, don't say it. You're getting mighty close to the null and void. Well, here we are, Jean Chelton. How do you like it?"

He pointed to a high-fronted car, easily thirty years old, that was parked near the curb; then stood back, waiting. There was something in his face that suggested both pride and humility.

Jean surveyed the car. It was what Bill would have called an ancient heap, but she knew better than to say anything like that to Andy. It's his own, she thought. He's probably paying for it out of the money he makes at the supermarket. And I bet he's a steady customer at Auto-Junk. If he's like Bill, he's spent hours, even whole days, on it. She cocked her head to one side. "You've done a beautiful paint job," she said. "It's really smooth, Andy. I can hardly wait to see how she runs."

She'd said the right thing. The humility was gone. Only the pride remained as Andy sprang forward to assist her over the door. "The lock's jimmied," he said. "A little hard to get into this thing."

Once he was inside, he patted the door on his side lovingly. "There's something about this old crate," he said. "When I'm in her, I always feel as though I'm sitting on top of the world."

Jean giggled. "I can understand that."

"Hey, no belittling."

"I'm not. Truly. But you've got to admit we *are* a little high off the ground."

"Yep. That's what my mom says. She gets dizzy. She's kind of cute, though. She's got a song that fits the way I feel. It's an oldie, you understand, but it goes like this." Unexpectedly Andy was singing. "I'm sitting on top of the world, just dreaming along, just singing a song."

"Why, I've heard my *own* mother sing that."

"Really?" He looked at her with astonishment. She stared back, and Andy looked away. He seemed a little embarrassed. "Well," he said. "This isn't getting us out to Miller's very fast, is it?"

He fiddled with the ignition, the starter, and, finally, the choke. He slid his left hand upward on the wheel and leaned forward, listening intently to the sound of the motor taking fire, and it was then that Jean noticed, for the first time, the ring on the third finger. It was his own ring! Not Georgia's, for he'd worn hers on his little finger. Hers had been a class ring, for she had been a senior, but Andy, as a junior, had been unable to give Georgia anything but this same onyx.

Her joy was instantaneous. Why hadn't she thought to look? Here she'd been worrying and wondering and all the time the reassurance she'd needed was right there!

The happiness of knowing could not be contained, and the resultant sigh was so deep that Andy turned questioningly. "Anything wrong?" He saw the direction of her gaze. "Oh. That. Yep, it's my own."

"Then you and Georgia—?"

"Georgia and I have had it."

"When, Andy?"

"Two weeks ago. Just before she went to the lake with her folks."

"I'm sorry."

"Are you, Jean?"

She was honest. "No, not really."

He grinned. "That's good. I'm kind of glad you're not. Because then you must—" he stopped, hit by a new thought. "If you're not, how come the heavy sigh a moment ago?"

Jean squirmed. "Well, I was afraid—I mean, I thought—I mean, after all—"

"Why, Jean Chelton, ma'am," he drawled. His tone held a teasing twang. "I do believe you-all thought I was goin' to take you aout, while all the time back home in the maountins I had a staidy girl."

Jean giggled. "You, sir, are so right."

"What's more," he said, "thinkin' all that, even so you were agoin' to go, weren't you?"

"Yes, ma'am, I mean, sir, I was."

"That's what gits me," he said. "It don't rightly seem you would have done that unless—"

His eyes dared her to finish the sentence. But she wouldn't. Not now. Some time, maybe. For now, it was enough to know that she was with him; that she had a right to be with him. The road to Miller's was merely a beginning. It *could* lead far beyond.

CHAPTER TWO

Hey," Andy said. It was twenty minutes later and, with a great screeching of brakes and a last final bang of the muffler, they had gunned to a stop. He looked around the parking area of Miller's with amazement. "What do you know? There's nobody here!"

Jean giggled. "What about the little girls in that car over there? And what about—isn't that Miss Henderson and her mother in the one beyond?"

Andy smote his forehead. "Not Miss Henderson! Don't we get enough English in the winter without being exposed in July? Look at her! What do you bet, she's sitting there this very minute conjugating verbs? Besides, you know what I meant. None of the *kids* are here."

"Did you want them to be?"

He looked at her. Ever since leaving the "Y" his chatter had been light and threaded with laughter. But now his voice was serious. "I'm not sure. Did you?"

She considered. "I don't know." Then she smiled. "Maybe we'd better claim the fifth amendment."

Andy grinned. "Maybe we'd better. No. Let's order something and then talk. What'll it be? You are limited," he pulled out his wallet and counted change, "to exactly twenty-three cents' worth of anything you see advertised on yon Miller's sign."

Jean unsnapped the "mad" money purse on her belt. "I've got—"

"Don't you dare," Andy said. "Don't you ever let me hear you offering to help pay for your own soda, young lady. That's my department. At times, you'll probably starve, but that's the way it is, that's the way it's got to be."

"Yes, sir, I mean no, sir, I mean I won't. And I'll have a root beer, please." She was glad he felt the way he did. She thought: Going out with someone for the first time is a funny thing. It's a kind of not knowing, but getting to. Andy's a lot the way I thought he would be, but he's different, too.

"Well," Andy said, after the car hop had brought them their drinks, "here's to the girl that just saved me eight cents." He lifted his cup and his eyes, over the rim, were teasing. "Here's to Jean Chelton, age sixteen, height about five-five, weight—better skip that, eyes blue, hair like the girl in the song, mouth kissable—*what* am I saying?" He drained the waxed container, placed it on the door-suspended tray, and leaned close, inspecting. "It *is*, you know."

Jean was flustered. She, too, put her container down; then, afraid that he might take the gesture as an invitation, picked it up again. "Please—I—you—" This was going too fast. She didn't know what to say.

12

He was, suddenly, penitent. "Hey, stop looking as though I'd just beaten you! It was a compliment, Jeannie. I didn't mean to—lots of girls would have—gosh, I'm sorry."

The first time out, she thought, is a kind of not knowing for the boy, too. The thought gave her confidence. "It's all right," she said. "Besides, it isn't my own mouth, you know. It's by courtesy of Revlon."

His laughter was spontaneous. It was impossible not to laugh along with him. They didn't stop laughing until they became conscious that one of the cars, in leaving the lot, had stopped beside them. A middle-aged woman leaned out. "Good evening, Andrew. Good evening, Jean."

"Good evening, Miss Henderson," they chorused.

"A little laughter does make the world go round, doesn't it?" the woman said.

Andy almost choked, but Jean managed to gasp a reply. "Yes, Miss Henderson, it certainly does."

The woman nodded and drove away.

"I laugh, you laugh, he laughs," Andy said.

"We laugh," Jean began, and got no further. Both of them were off again.

Later, spent, they looked at each other. "What hit us?" Jean asked. "As Miss Henderson herself might say, that was certainly much ado about nothing."

"Or—laugh and the world laughs with you," Andy said. "Weep and—gosh, Jean, I'm glad you're not the weeping kind. Georgia was always—"

So real was the thought of her that, at the mention of her name, the girl herself might have been sitting between them. For an instant Jean saw her vividly—saw the lithe, sun-browned figure, the blue, slanted eyes, the hair that reflected hours of care, and that this year was tinted pale gold.

"I shouldn't have mentioned her," Andy said. "But since I have, I think I'd better get things straight with you. I don't want you to think—you aren't just another girl, Jean. I've been wanting to date you for a long time."

"Have you?"

"Sure. A few months ago, I even tried to break with Georgia, without letting her know why, of course. But Georgia didn't want to. Not then, anyway, and when a guy's been going with a girl for two years—well, gosh, he can't let her down just whammo!"

"And so?"

"And so we just kept on. But we didn't get along too well. We were always fighting. I honestly think that if it hadn't been for the prom coming up, Georgia would have ditched me sooner than she did."

This was news. "But I thought—"

"Yeah, I thought, too. Big-headed dope that I was, I figured I was indispensable. But in the end, it was Georgia who wrote 'finish.' Some joke, huh?"

"No. It's not funny."

"I guess not." Andy flexed his hands on the wheel. "Well, anyway, it's all over between us. Period. Kaput."

"Are you sure? Georgia is—she's awfully pretty."

He seemed startled by her comment. He said, after a moment, "Say, you're a regular guy, aren't you?"

"Why?"

"You could have said something catty about her. A lot of girls would have. Sure, she's pretty, but she's not for me. Know why?"

Her "no" was soft, because she was thinking "yes." Or, at least, hoping.

"Because of you. I like you, Jean."

That, Jean thought, makes us even. "I like you, too," she said, and wondered if she was making the admission too soon.

"Good." His mood changed. He chuckled. "We sound like charter members of the D.C.M.A. Society. Hey, how about that?"

"What's the D.C. and I forget the rest of it society?"

"Decker-Chelton-Mutual-Admiration. What else?"

"It sounds organized. And we're not."

"A small item. We'll take care of that as of now." He banged the container on the tray. "As senior member of the D.C.M.A. society, I hereby declare that the first meeting is in session. Does the junior member have any business to present?"

Jean laughed. This was fun. *Andy* was fun, just as she'd known he would be. "Yes, sir. Why do I have to be the junior member?"

"Chelton, you shock me. You have to be the junior

14

member because you're a girl. A girl is known as one of the lesser sex. It follows, therefore, that, as the only other member of this board, I, naturally, must exercise my male prerogative and assume full duties and responsibilities of senior member, thereby allowing to fall upon you—"

"All the work of this organization, I bet," Jean interrupted. "Okay, Decker, I get it."

Andy looked at her from the corners of his eyes. "And now that we have settled the point under question, is there any further business on the agenda?"

"No, sir. I have nothing more to offer."

"Chelton, I can see you have not been giving this matter proper thought."

"Lack of time. I bow to the senior member."

"Who, in turn, bows to the junior member." And he did. It was a very complicated bow, since it had to be accomplished around a driving wheel and while sitting, but Andy managed it.

"You," Jean said, "are a clown."

He sat up, adopting a hurt expression. "This meeting is fast going beyond control. I seem to detect a note of hilarity that is not properly respectful. Therefore, I shall entertain a motion that the first meeting of the D.C.M.A. be dismissed, the second meeting to be held—" His face became a little anxious. "Tomorrow, Jean?"

Tomorrow. He wanted to see her tomorrow. She had made the grade. "Tomorrow will be fine."

"Good. About eight? We can ram around in Old Faithful or go to a movie or something."

"Sounds like fun."

"It will be. That's a promise. And now," he glanced at his watch, "I'd better get you home. I don't want to get started wrong with your parents."

He pressed the horn, and while the car hop was removing the trays, Jean took a long, last look at Miller's. Through the windows she could see the short counter, with the small packages of cheese crackers and the Saran-wrapped cookies crowding the cash register. She noted the food preparation counter beyond and watched the waitress leaning tiredly against a huge metal coffee urn, sipping slowly from a paper cup. I never before realized, she thought, that her uniform is blue. Or that the chef's cap

15

has *Miller's* written across it that way. Or that there are only six booths in the inside eating area. Or that railroad tracks run in back of the place. Or that the building on the right is a house and the one on the left is a varnish factory. But I'll always remember now. I'll remember because this is where I came with Andy the very first time we were together.

She was rather quiet on the way home. She kept wishing that Miller's were located thirty miles from town instead of five. It would mean that much more time with the boy beside her. The boy himself was quiet, too, although occasionally he turned his face briefly to smile companionably at her.

When they parked in front of the house, he turned off the ignition and faced her, resting his arm across the back of the seat. "I'm glad you live on a hill, Jean. There are times when I've got to start this blasted boat in gear."

"Bill had a car, once, that he had to start with a crank."

His face was alive with interest. "He did? I'd like to see it."

"He hasn't got it, any more. Oh, he may still have a part or two lying around. He was always tinkering. He paid twenty dollars for the whole thing, originally, and we kept telling him that he'd paid good money for the privilege of lying on his back—something he could have done for free."

"Yes, but a car with a crank! Gosh!" Andy's tone was one of reverence.

"You sound just like him."

"I'd like to meet him."

"You will. My Mom and Dad, too. And speaking of parents, I'd better get out. They don't like it when I sit in a car in front of the house." She thought, saying it, isn't it funny that I don't mind telling him? Getting from the car to the house is one of the things that's always bothered me, with other boys. With Andy, though, it seems perfectly natural. I wonder if it's because our mothers know the same song.

He said, as they walked to the door, "What are you smiling about?"

"Was I smiling? I didn't know."

"You certainly were. You looked like a politician lis-

16

tening to the applause for his own speech."

"An apt description. I was feeling benevolent."

"And, obviously, you're not going to answer my question. Okay, keep your secrets."

Two lamps were on in the living room, but no one was there. Jean stopped just inside the door. "Everyone's gone to bed, I guess. Well—" She hesitated. She'd never been very good at "good-nights" and she was wondering if he would kiss her. She hoped, in a strange, breathless, hardly daring to admit it way, that he would.

He didn't. He said, "Your hair's out of place again." As lightly as he'd done it before, he brushed it back. "Good night, Jeannie Chelton."

"Good night, Andy Decker."

That was all. It was better than a kiss. It was absolutely perfect.

When he was gone, she whirled around the room and threw herself on the sofa with such joy that the springs creaked. She got up immediately and went to the mirror at the foot of the stairs—not to check on herself as herself, but as the girl Andy had seen. But she was too excited to do an evaluation. And there was not time. Her mother's voice was calling from upstairs. "Is that you, Jean?"

"Yes."

"We've all gone to bed. Will you see that the lights are turned off, dear?"

"Okay, Mom."

She turned them off and, even though it was dark, took the stairs two at a time, falling halfway to the top.

"Jean, are you all right?" The voice came as expected.

"All right, Mom?" Jean got to her feet and continued more slowly. "I most certainly am." She paused by her mother's door. "I've never been so all right in my life! But don't ask me why. Because I don't intend to tell you until tomorrow."

Tomorrow. Magic word in a magic world. Tomorrow and tomorrow and tomorrow. And Andy and Andy and Andy . . .

CHAPTER THREE

He called her at noon the next day. She'd been lying on a beach towel in the back yard, and her legs, arms, and back were shiny with baby oil. When the phone rang she jumped to her feet and upset the bottle of iodine she always mixed with the oil for promoting a proper shade of tan. She said, "Oh, darn!" but she didn't have time to mop it up. The phone was still ringing, and it *might* be Andy. She'd already talked with Virginia. She raced into the house.

It was Andy. "Hi," he said.

"Hi."

"You sound out of breath."

"I am. I was in the yard. Sun bathing."

"Wish I could see you."

"I'm glad you can't. My hair's all done up in pink roll-on clamps and I've got grease on my face and I just spilled iodine all over everything and—"

"And if you're trying to disillusion me, you're doing a mighty good job. Look, I've only got a few minutes. I'm on my lunch break. But I thought you should know. We're headline news."

"I figured we would be. I saw the kids looking at us when we left the Y last night."

"The word got around this morning. Apparently we were too late for the seven star final, but we certainly made the early morning edition. Grubholz must've been on the phone at dawn. At least six kids have stopped in the supermarket today. They all want the same thing."

"Bread? Corn flakes?"

"No, goon. They all want to know is it true."

"And what do you say?"

"I tell them the truth. It *is* true, isn't it? I *did* take you home last night, didn't I? I *do* have a date with you tonight, don't I? I'm *not* dreaming, am I?"

"Yes, yes, yes, and yes. No, I mean, no. To the last, I

18

mean. Yes, to the others." Suddenly she laughed. "Do you follow me?"

His answering laughter came back to her. "How could I? I haven't got my code book handy. Listen, I've got to go. I'll see you tonight. 'Bye, now."

The telephone was in the kitchen. After Jean had hung up, she walked to the work counter by the sink, where her mother was cutting celery. Jean picked up a whole stalk and bit reflectively. "What's for lunch?"

"Tuna fish salad." Mrs. Chelton glanced at her daughter and said, "We'll be eating in about ten minutes. You can help me set the table, but you'd better get some of that oil off you first."

Jean didn't move. "It's Betty's turn to set the table."

"Your sister isn't here. She's been playing with Martha Johnson all morning and they're going to eat in the Johnsons' back-yard tent."

"Oh, well, I don't mind. It won't hurt me, I guess."

Mrs. Chelton looked quizzical. She was a pleasant-faced woman in her mid-forties, but she had the figure, William Chelton, Senior, often said, of a young girl. "A little heavy around the middle, you understand," he always added. "But I've seen a few heads turn." To which his wife would respond, "Stop turning mine, then."

Jean knew that she was lucky in her parents. Perhaps the best description of them was what one of her friends had once said. "Your mother and father are really tops. Most parents lump kids our ages into a bracket labeled 'teen-age.' It's what we are, of course, but it's the way they say it. As though we were a strange species—with sub-zero mentalities and no rights of our own. They never see us as individuals, the way your parents do."

Now Mrs. Chelton said, "Well, that's a new twist. You mean you're going to give in without a struggle?"

"Give what in?" Jean asked dreamily.

Her mother chuckled. "Is he really that nice?"

"Who?"

"That boy you're thinking about."

"Andy Decker? He's—" Jean came to. When she saw the way her mother was smiling, she smiled back. "He's really that nice. We have a date tonight. I can hardly wait for you to meet him."

19

"Time will fly," her mother said. "It's flying right now. And the table still isn't set."

"Oh. Sorry. Wait till I get this stuff off. I'll be right back." Jean headed for the back stairs. "By the way, Mom, what are we having for lunch?"

Her mother looked at her. She didn't reply. She merely shook her head.

Jean didn't set the table, after all. They ate in the yard. Her mother said, when she came downstairs, "William called. He took the car in for repairs this morning and the garage won't be finished with it until about two o'clock. He said he'd get a bite downtown. And this is the week Bill carries his lunch, so there will be just the two of us. Shall we try the lilac tree?"

Jean nodded and began fixing their trays. This was something she and her mother and Betty, too, loved to do in the summer. They seldom had the chance, for neither of the men in the family enjoyed tray meals. Mr. Chelton said that he could never keep the confounded plates from sliding, and Bill complained that a guy didn't have a place to put his legs.

For a lilac, the tree was immense, and its shade was pleasant. Jean said, "This is nice. I feel sorry for Bill, working in that old factory. The heat must be terrific."

"I'm sure it is," her mother replied. "But Bill takes it in stride, and the money he's getting will help a lot toward his last year in college. He didn't make nearly as much last summer, when he had that road job."

"He got a better tan, though."

Her mother smiled. "Well, as long as we manage one good tan in the family. We've got two, really. Betty's running you a close second, and she's not even trying. Would you look at those two tykes right now?"

Three yards down, two small figures were walking carefully toward the pup tent at the end of the lot. They were carrying plates of food and glasses of milk, and their heads were bent, watching for hazards.

"Wouldn't you think," Jean said, "they'd suffocate in that tent?"

"You didn't. Not when *you* were nine."

"So I didn't. And the tent Virginia and I used wasn't

20

even a tent. It was a bunch of blankets hung over a card table."

They ate slowly, relaxing. A feeling of laziness and drowsiness captured them. Finished, Mrs. Chelton put her tray to one side. "I'm going to scandalize the neighbors. I'm going to roll over on my stomach and sleep, and to heck with the dishes."

"I'll do them," Jean said. "Later." She lay on her back, with her arm over her eyes. Andy, she thought.

Andy. She remembered the first time she'd been conscious of him as Andy Decker. She'd been in the guidance counselor's office and when she'd come out, he was sitting on the bench against the wall, waiting his turn. He'd smiled at her and that had been that. She'd felt the lurch within her, and she'd thought she couldn't wait until she found out what Virginia knew about him. For Virginia would know. She knew everything about everybody. She was a regular computation machine.

Virginia hadn't disappointed her. "Well," she'd said. "He seems like a good kid. You know, of course, that he doesn't play football or basketball or any of those things. I don't think he does anything outstanding in the way of grades, either. But then, I suppose he doesn't have time. His father's dead and he and his mother have a pretty rough time of it. She works in the office at Dow's. Typist or secretary or something. Andy works at Loblaw's after school and on Saturdays. I thought you would have known that."

"We do our marketing at Quaker."

"Oh. Well, that's about it, I guess. Except for one very important thing. He goes steady with Georgia Kane. So you might as well forget him."

They were walking home from school and the wind was high. But it wasn't the wind that caused Jean to shiver. It was the thought of Georgia Kane. Still, Georgia was a senior. She'd be going away next year. Andy, like herself, was a junior. Next year held promise.

She watched for him, after that. In the halls, and during assemblies, and at Grandy's, the local hangout, although she saw him there only once. She did see him on Friday nights, though, at Teen-Inn. Always with Georgia.

21

Everlastingly with Georgia. So she danced with Leroy and with Freddy and with Virginia and Susy and kept hoping. Once, when her mother sent her for groceries, she stopped at Loblaw's, but another boy helped carry her bags to the car.

Several times during the spring she *had* thought he was watching her. She noticed it particularly right after his supposed remark to Barney. Had he really said that? Some time she would ask him. In view of what had happened last night it seemed likely. It was such a happy thought to know that all the time she had been wanting to date him, he had been wanting to go out with her. It was as though for months they had been sharing a secret, but hadn't known they were sharing it until just now. Maybe Andy still didn't know—she hadn't told him as much as he'd told her. But *she* knew, and the knowledge gave her a delicious bubbling feeling. Last night had made all the waiting worth while. And tonight—well, tonight would be even better.

What should she wear? He wouldn't expect a skirt, would he? Surely, hot as it was, shorts would be best. Unless they went to the movies. Maybe she'd better call Virginia.

Her mother made no move as Jean gathered up the trays and went quietly toward the house. Virginia's line was busy the first time, but the second try brought results. She was home, thank goodness, and she had the answer.

"Wear your shorts, dope. The white ones. With a blue blouse. But have your white wrap-around ready, just in case."

Of course. It was unbelievably simple.

Not too simple, she learned. At seven o'clock that evening her clothes were ready but Jean wasn't. She stood in the upstairs hall and banged on the bathroom door. "Bill Chelton, come out of there."

"Can't." Her brother's voice was infuriatingly lazy. "I'm shaving."

"Well, the very minute you're through—"

"The minute I'm through I'm going to perform the second S."

"You mean you haven't showered yet? Oh, Bill! Please let me have the bathroom!"

"Sorry. I've got to shampoo this grimy old head."

"You and your three S's! Couldn't you skip one of them for a change?"

"Nope. I've got a heavy date!"

"Well, so have I!"

The door opened a crack and a grinning, belathered face peered out. "At your age, Miss Chelton? You're still in the lightweight class!"

She started toward him. "Bill Chelton, if you don't—"

He chuckled, and quickly withdrew his head. She heard the bolt sliding on the other side of the door. "O sole mio," he sang. "La da, dee, da. O sole mio, da da, dee, dum."

From behind Jean came another voice. "What's a heavy date?"

Jean whirled in exasperation. *"This* family! As if it isn't enough to have a brother who ties up the bathroom, I've got to have a sister who—" She relented when she saw Betty's stricken face and, leaning down, kissed the top of the little girl's Dutch-cut hair. "I'm sorry, honey. Come on in my bedroom and talk with me while I wait for that darned Bill to get out of there."

"All right." Clutching a limp stuffed dog tightly to her thin figure, Betty sat on the floor and watched Jean at the dressing table. "What shall we talk about?"

"Oh, I don't know."

"Would you rather play a game? Like 'I see something yellow'?"

"Not now."

"Why are you smiling at yourself in the mirror?"

Jean, caught, flushed slightly. "I was smiling at you, pudding."

"But I'm way over here," the little girl pointed out; then, with no seeming transition, went on in the same matter-of-fact tone. "Who's Andy Decker?"

"Why, he's the boy—" Suddenly Jean looked closely at her sister. "How did *you* know about Andy Decker?"

"I heard Mom ask Dad if he knew him."

"Oh. Well, I'll tell you. He's the boy I'm going out with tonight."

"Do you like him?"

"Yes."

"Is he pretty?"

Jean giggled. "Boys aren't pretty, sweetheart."

"Bill is. He's—"

"Bill's what?" The owner of the name, wrapped in a huge towel, appeared in the doorway. He bowed in Jean's direction. "The b.r., Mademoiselle Chelton, is all yours. I'll wait for my shower, since this is obviously a big night in your life."

"Bill, you're a doll. Pretty, too. Ask Betty, if you don't think so." She ducked, then, to avoid the wet washcloth that was coming straight toward her face.

At ten minutes to eight, Jean was walking down the stairs to the living room. She paused on the third from the bottom step, to point-check herself in the mirror that hung on the facing wall. Shoes, plain, one point. Shorts, one color, one point. Contrasting blouse, one point. Circle pin on collar, one point. Dull silver bracelet, souvenir of an Indian gift shop, one point. She'd do. She was five points under the maximum; but then, she usually was. Not for her the bows, necklaces, fancy shoes, and clutter that some girls wore. She was, she'd long ago decided, the tailored type. Virginia had agreed, up to a point. "The funny thing is," she'd said, "that even in shorts and slacks, you still manage to look like a girl."

Did she look like a girl now? Yes. And why not? She felt like a girl. A girl who was going out with a very special boy.

She looked around the living room. How would Andy see it? Would he compare it with the one in the Kanes' home? She hoped not. The Cheltons couldn't compete with the interior decorator influence so obvious there. The Cheltons ran to rather worn rugs, and white ruffled curtains, and comfortable chairs. There was never complete orderliness, but always a magazine left on the floor, a pile of books on a table, someone's hat on an ottoman. Right now Jean's father was sitting in his favorite chair, with newspaper sheets strewn around him. He was reading and watching a ball game on television at one and the same time. He glanced up. "How's my favorite older daughter tonight?"

She sat on the arm of his chair and rumpled his hair, the same light brown as her own, the same light brown as

24

that of all the Chelton children. "Fine. What's the score?"

"Three to two in favor of the Pirates."

"Good. I'm glad they're ahead."

"Too close. They need a few more insurance runs."

She leaned around him, inspecting his concerned face. "As Mom says, don't worry. You don't own any stock in the club."

He grinned, his eyes crinkling at the corners. "Too risky."

The doorbell rang. Mr. Chelton laid his paper aside and got to his feet as Jean ushered Andy into the room.

"Andy, I want you to meet my father. Dad, this is Andy Decker."

Her father and Andy shook hands, and Andy stood a moment, uncertainly. Then, "How's the game going, sir?" he asked.

"The Pirates are leading."

"Good."

Mr. Chelton shot an appreciative glance at the boy and Jean was glad that they were rooting for the same team.

"Sit down," Mr. Chelton said, "and watch for a few minutes. That second baseman they brought up from the farm team is on deck."

"Thanks," Andy said. "I haven't seen him yet, but he certainly has a good record."

He sat on the first chair inside the door and stretched long legs, encased in clean slacks, before him. His shoes, Jean noted, were half-soled, but they were polished. His white, short-sleeved sport shirt was immaculate, and his dark hair showed signs of recent wetting.

Mrs. Chelton came into the room. "I thought I heard—oh, hello." She smiled at Andy, who immediately jumped to his feet.

Jean performed introductions and again they all sat, only to have Bill come bounding down the stairs, whistling. This, Jean thought, must really be an ordeal. I'm glad we don't have visiting grandparents.

Ten minutes later Jean knew that something was wrong. She couldn't quite figure what, except that it had something to do with Bill, and the way he kept looking at Andy. He seemed in no hurry to leave, either, and she was sure that he was already late for his date with Maggie.

About the middle of the fourth inning Bill said, and his remark had nothing to do with the baseball they'd all been watching so intently, "I've seen you around, haven't I, Decker?"

"I don't know. Probably."

"I've been trying to think where."

Jean said. "If you haven't run across each other in auto supply stores, it's a miracle."

Bill's manner showed, at last, more warmth. "Like cars, Decker?"

"Sure do. The older the better. Jean was telling me last night about the crank model you had once. What was it—a model T?"

"A 1919 Studebaker. Touring."

"Wow! Where'd you find her?"

"In a barn. Some old guy had kept her jacked up for a couple of decades. She was a sweet job."

"I'll bet."

Bill said nothing more. Once again he seemed to be studying Andy, but finally, almost reluctantly, he got to his feet. "I guess I'll have to shove. Maggie will throttle me if I don't show pretty soon."

"She should," Mrs. Chelton said. "Any boy who would keep a nice girl like Maggie Phillipson waiting—"

Bill stood where he was. Suddenly he turned to Jean. "Maggie and I are going to the drive-in. I think you two ought to come with us."

What a suggestion! Jean thought. Didn't Bill know that on her first date with Andy she wanted to be alone with him? "Thanks," she said. "But some other time. We're going to—" She looked at Andy questioningly.

Andy looked uncomfortable. "I'd thought swimming, maybe," he said. "But we can go with Bill if you'd like."

"Swimming sounds wonderful. So give us a rain check," she paused and made deliberate use of a phrase that Bill would understand, "brother of mine."

It was a signal and Bill got it. Whatever was wrong, they would talk it over later.

Bill said, "Okay, then. See you tomorrow." He didn't look very pleased, but he left.

Andy and Jean left, too, after Jean had gathered her suit and towel, and after Andy's awkward "See you" to her parents. Once outside, he breathed deeply, probably in relief that inspection was over.

But it wasn't, quite. Betty and Martha Johnson and six or seven other small fry, in assorted shapes and sizes, were playing "Fair Trade" in the front yard. They stood in two parallel rows, facing one another, but as Andy and Jean appeared, they stopped, as though on signal, and stared solemnly.

Martha said, "Who's that with your sister, Betty?"

"That's Andy Decker."

"Who's he?"

"He," Betty said importantly, "is a heavy date."

CHAPTER FOUR

Andy's car jolted along the unpaved road that led to Roddy's Pond, three miles from town. Many times, when she was younger, Jean had walked the entire distance. Once, when she'd been working for a badge, she had come this way with two eager Girl Scouts, and at six o'clock in the morning they had built a fire and fixed bacon and eggs. Another time, in seventh grade, the whole class had hiked to the pond for a picnic, and one of the girls had almost drowned.

"This road," she said to Andy, "brings back memories."

"Jean Chelton, don't tell me you're so old you're living in the past already! Wake up and live. This is now!"

"I know." This was now, she thought, but even this would be a memory by tomorrow. She didn't say it. She didn't know Andy well enough. "I haven't been this way for some time, and I guess I couldn't help remembering. Virginia and Susy and I used to think that escaped convicts always hid out in these summer camps along here."

Andy laughed. "Escaped convicts? Here? What an imagination!"

"Sounds crazy, doesn't it? But we did. There's a camp

around the next bend that is sort of decrepit and run-down, and even in broad daylight, with the sun shining, we used to run past it."

"Well, I'll be darned! Come to think of it, I used to get scared coming here, too. Not of convicts. Of rattlers. Boy! The day Tom Evans found a dried-up snake skin on the road, you'd have thought we'd been turned loose in a den of the blasted things! Tom kept saying, 'Who's going to suck the blood when one of us gets bit?'"

"Not really?"

"Sure, really."

"Kids certainly get funny ideas, don't they?"

"Mixed up. I wouldn't be a kid again for anything."

"Why not?"

"Oh, I don't know. Being a kid, for me, anyway, was no fun. Darn!" Andy swerved the car to avoid a rut in the road, but was unsuccessful. His knees hit the steering wheel. "These old cars don't have enough leg room."

She'd noticed that, last night. "Bill used to complain of the same thing."

"Bill," Andy repeated. "You know, I got the feeling that your brother wasn't exactly taken with me."

She'd had the same feeling but now she denied it. "Of course he was. You've got a lot in common."

"Maybe. I didn't know he went with Maggie Phillipson. Steady?"

"No."

"You mean he's a free wheeler?"

"No, he just goes with Maggie. But he's got another year in college, and he says it isn't fair to her."

"Why not, if she likes him?"

"Because he's away, and she's here. She works, you know. She took a secretarial course after high school, one of those two-year deals. She's got a good job with Kraft and Eakin."

"The lawyers."

"Don't let them hear you speak of them that way. Maggie says they've got to be called attorneys."

"Attorneys, then. But if she works, so what? It seems to me that—oh, well, it's none of my business."

He said, a few minutes later, "How do you think I did with your parents?"

28

"They liked you."

"I hope so. Gosh, I certainly was scared! Do you think, now that they've met me, they'll let you go out again?"

"They let me tonight, didn't they?"

"Yeah, but—" He scowled comically. "How about you? Are you willing to go out with a disreputable character like me?"

"If you want me to."

"If I want you to? Are you being coy? Don't you know?"

"I wanted to hear you say it."

Right in the middle of the road he stopped the car. "Chelton, I'll do better than that. I'll put it in writing." He traced invisible words on the windshield. "Now, do you know?"

"I couldn't tell what you wrote."

He grinned. "Too bad you're so illiterate. You'll just have to guess." He started the car again.

Neither of them spoke for a time. Then Andy said, "Beautiful night, isn't it?"

"Yes."

It was. The moon was up, and the trees and bushes on either side of the road were softly outlined. The planks of the old bridge over Beaver Creek rattled as they drove across, and from below came the sound of water tumbling over rocks into the deeper currents of Roddy's Pond. A number of people were ahead of them. There were three fires on the pebble beach, the smell of charred frankfurters, the sound of laughter, of singing.

Andy parked the car among the bushes and gestured toward the path that led up over the hill. "You get ready first. I'll wait here."

She'd wondered about the problem of getting into her suit. There were no dressing rooms, only bushes and trees and sky and a locked pumphouse. She'd never come here before with a boy, except for the classic occasion of the seventh-grade outing. That time, though there had been boys as well as girls, there had also been a teacher with a bent for organization. She'd been afraid of embarrassment at this moment, but now it seemed perfectly natural to saunter up the path, find a well screened spot, climb quickly into her suit, and stroll back. She tossed her

29

clothes into the back seat of Andy's car. "Your turn."

Waiting, she walked onto the bridge, leaned on the railing, and stared below. Not too many people. Not even anyone she knew. Good. She didn't want to share Andy tonight. She'd thought, for a few minutes at home, that she might have to. Bill had had a very stubborn look about him. What had got into him? Usually he was friendly. Tolerant sometimes, and occasionally amused, but friendly. Oh, why worry? She'd have it out with him tomorrow. No sense in letting the thought of him spoil this night with Andy. Andy was so dear. He was so much fun to be with. Had Georgia thought so, too? Georgia. Was Andy comparing her with Georgia? She hoped not. She couldn't compete with Georgia. Georgia had everything. Even her own private telephone line. Georgia would die before she'd swim in a muddy old hole like Roddy's, though. Of course, Georgia wasn't alone in this. Most of the teen-agers seldom came here. If they wanted to go swimming, they used the pool at Launee, the town park. But Andy hadn't mentioned Launee, he'd brought her here. Maybe, just maybe, he felt as she did about tonight.

"Angel?" Andy's voice, right beside her, caused her to jump.

"Sorry," he said. "I thought you heard me. Are you ready to go down?"

The sight of him, clad only in swimming trunks, was so unsettling that she could hear a sudden pounding in her ears. It wasn't just that he was thin—it was, oh, seeing his ribs, and—and—hair on his chest, and the muscular look of his legs—

She was caught in a wave of feeling like nothing she had ever before experienced. She wanted only to run. And she did. She headed for the footpath on the steep bank that led to the water, and half walked, half slid, over the dried mud and pebbles. She slipped near the bottom and fell, bruising her thigh. But she was up immediately, racing for the water. Then she was swimming—fast, faster, over to the far side. She climbed out on a rock and shook water from her ears, from her eyes. She looked, then, for Andy.

He was still on the other side. He was entering the water cautiously and he was not, she noted, a very good swimmer.

30

What had happened to her? Why had she run from him? There was no time to search for an answer. He was directly beneath the rock; he was pulling himself up beside her. "Wow!" he gasped. "You certainly run a guy a race!" He lay back, then, and closed his eyes.

She sat beside him, cradling her knees in her arms, contemplating, but not seeing, the moon. He said, after a moment, "Got it all figured out?"

"Got what figured out?"

"What makes the world go round."

She smiled suddenly. "Laughter."

He sat up. "You're quoting."

"So I am." She looked at him. Why had she felt so funny a few minutes ago? This was Andy. He wasn't a stranger. He was the boy who studied English under the same teacher she did. "You know something?" she said. "I feel wonderful. Absolutely, positively, marvelously, superabundantly wonderful. Let's go in again, shall we?"

He made a wry face. "Demon for punishment. All right, Chelton. Only this time, let's go together."

They swam for perhaps half an hour. Andy found a heavy rope suspended from a tree near the water's edge and, emitting Tarzanlike cries, swung himself out over the pond, dropping off near the middle. Jean surface dived and practiced her back stroke and allowed Andy to duck her occasionally. Not too much, just enough to make up for the fact that she beat him in the one short race they tried.

He said finally, "Chelton, you're too good for me. I'm pooped."

"So'm I, Decker," she fibbed. "I'm—so tired—I can hardly—speak. You get dressed first. While I—catch —my breath."

When he came back he was carrying a carton of soft drinks. "I forgot these," he said. "I was going to put 'em in the stream to keep cold. I hope you like your root beer tepid."

Root beer! How perfectly dear of him to remember! She hugged the thought to her as she dressed. Last night had meant something to him, too. As tonight . . .

They built their own fire, away from the few others. No one was in the water now. Roddy's Pond was a world within a world. A small world, bounded by glowing fires, shadowy figures, and star-hung sky. A world in which the sounds were the low, indistinct ones of human voices, the decisive, haunting ones of woodland creatures, the mesmerizing one of water traveling now swiftly, now lazily, toward a known river, an unknown sea.

They talked. And were still. And talked again.

Andy told her of the time his father died, and of how, since the age of seven, he had considered himself as the man of the house. He told her of the last time he had cried. He'd been nine, then, and he'd solved the puzzle in the colored supplement of the Sunday paper, only to find that he hadn't actually won a pony, only the chance to sell candy on a punch-the-ticket basis. He told her of his early paper route, and of his Saturday work, the preceding year, as a grease monkey. He spoke with pride of his present job. "It's hard, but I'm lucky to have it. For kids my age, it's the best paying one in town."

Jean, listening, felt pride herself. No wonder he doesn't swim well, she thought. He's never had a chance for much fun. He's been too busy all his life, just working. It makes the accomplishments of kids like Freddy and Leroy and some of the rest seem small, by comparison.

By eleven o'clock the root beer was gone. Andy went to the stream, filled a bottle, and came back to the fire. He emptied the contents and watched the steam and smoke rising. "There! That's got it. Jean, I—"

He hesitated and she waited.

"Andy?"

"Nothing. We've got to get going."

They climbed the bank in silence and, still in silence, got into the car. Andy turned to her. "Jean, what I started to say back there—" He gestured with his head. "I just want you to know—well, I've never known another girl like you. This has been—it's only been the best night of my life, that's all. Go ahead. Laugh, if you want to."

"Laugh? Andy, look at me. Andy, I'm closer to crying than anything. I'm not sure why. It's just that tonight has been perfect, I guess. For me, as well as for you."

His look was of such genuine surprise that suddenly she found herself doing something she had never expected to do. She had never thought that she would be the one to take the initiative in kissing a boy, but now she was. She was kissing Andy Decker.

He didn't spoil it. He didn't grab her, or kiss her back. He looked at her for a long, hushed moment, and in his eyes she saw all that he was thinking.

It was enough.

CHAPTER FIVE

All right, Bill," Jean said. "Let's have it. What was the matter with you last night?"

It was seven o'clock in the evening and they were sitting on the back porch. The porch was small, and high, but the Chelton children had always preferred it to the front one. Probably, Bill had once said, between bites from a huge sandwich, because it was so close to the kitchen.

But it was more than that, Jean had decided. It was the feeling of privacy. Only old people liked to sit on front porches—to see and be seen, to say "Hot tonight, isn't it?" to passers-by. Or "I understand your grandchildren have come for a visit. Let me see, now, it's St. Mary's where they live, isn't it?"

Bill sat on a folding director's chair and propped his feet on the porch railing. His legs were long and made up a lot of what he always referred to as "six feet of Chelton." He'd have been greatly discomfited to know that he'd been variously labeled, depending upon the temperament of Jean's friends, as a doll, a lamb, a pro, a zoomer, a darling. That other girls applied such words to her brother had always amazed Jean.

They had an easy relationship. They had bickered over marble shooter ownership, they had measured pieces of cake to make sure the other didn't get the larger, they had called each other the worst names they could think of. Yet when Jean had scarlet fever, Bill had brought her his pitching glove, and when Bill had pneumonia, she'd read to him from her favorite book of poems and had never understood why he always went to sleep after the second stanza. She had caught him in his first experiment with shaving, and for weeks had held over him the threat of telling their father whose razor had been borrowed. He had caused her a whole night of tears by bringing one of his pals to the house when she was giving herself a home permanent. He could beat her at checkers, at tennis, at Ping-pong, but once she had caught a nineteen-inch bass when all he'd been able to pull out of the river was an insignificant little chub.

Through the years they'd laughed and cried, borrowed and paid back, quarreled and made up, conspired with and against, and had somehow arrived at the point where they not only liked, but respected each other.

Evidence of this respect was in Bill's manner now. He didn't look at Jean, though she was perched on the railing, facing him. He pulled a knife from his pocket, snapped open the blade, then closed it. "This Andy Decker. Where did you meet him?"

"He's in my class at school. Why?"

Again he snapped open the blade, and squinted along its edge. "Know him well?"

"Of course."

"Sure about that?"

"Yes. That is—no, I guess. You know how it is. We've got a large class."

"So you don't really know him? I mean, the kind of a guy he is?"

"What is this?" Jean asked. She was becoming angry. "Of course I know what kind of a guy he is. He is the kind of a guy I like. Do you think I'd have gone out with him if I didn't like him? Do you think I'd be going out with him again tomorrow? And every other time he asks me?"

"Simmer down," Bill said. "You aren't getting what I mean, at all."

"Just what do you mean, then?"

"Well," Bill shifted and the chair creaked. "Okay. I'll give it to you straight. Last night, as soon as I saw Andy Decker, I realized that there was something about him that I ought to know, something that I did know, but for a while I couldn't put my finger on it. And then, it dawned on me that he was the boy I'd seen one night up on Breck Hill with Georgia Kane."

Breck Hill. It was a parking spot, and the thought of Andy being there with Georgia was a sharp pain, to be dismissed now, but to be remembered later. The hurt in Jean's face was reflected in her voice as she said, "And what were *you* doing up on Breck Hill, *if* I may inquire?"

Bill squirmed. "Oh, Maggie and I were just riding around."

"I'll bet!"

"Okay. We were—well, gosh, Jean, Maggie and I are—we're—"

"Different from everybody else, I suppose."

"Yes, darn it, we are! Maggie's no Georgia Kane."

"And what is that supposed to mean?"

"That," Bill said, "is supposed to mean that I think you're too young and inexperienced to be going out with a boy who's been dating a girl like that!"

"Too young? Of all the—" Jean gasped. She leaned forward, almost toppling from the railing. Then, as she righted herself, the import of what he'd said hit. "And how does it happen that great big wise old you even knows that Georgia Kane exists? She's young, too, you know. Only a year older than I."

"Georgia Kane," Bill said firmly, "was never young. She was born old. Listen, Jean. I happen to know about Georgia because I'm a guy, and guys invariably know about girls like Georgia. Georgia has always traveled with an older crowd. She started dating eleventh graders when she was in eighth, and when I was a senior, and she was in her last year of junior high, a lot of the guys in my class took her out. A regular heartbreaker, Georgia. The thing that amazes me is that she wound up with a boy who is younger. Maybe it was inevitable, starting as early as she did."

"All *right!*" Jean said. "So, by your own admission, some of the guys your age have taken her out. Friends of yours, Methuselah?"

"Some of them."

"Nice guys?"

"Sure."

"Well? Just because Andy Decker is younger, does that

35

make him some kind of a—of a—" She searched for a descriptive word, could find none, and went on, "What *are* you trying to imply about him? So you saw him on Breck Hill with Georgia. So half the kids in town have parked there at one time or another, haven't they?"

"Have you?" Bill asked quickly.

"No. But that doesn't mean that I won't, maybe, some time."

"You'd better not let me catch you."

"Oh, Bill, don't be stuffy! What do you expect me to do—spend my whole life singing hymns?"

Bill grinned a little. "No. It's just that, at your age, parking can sometimes get out of hand."

"But not at yours?"

"I didn't say that. I guess, at any age, it can and, too darned many times, does. But, at least, when you're as old as I you've learned to guard against it. I mean, listen, Jean, the best way to avoid complications is to stay out of situations that might cause them. Maggie and I seldom park. Know why? Because we're in love. Sounds crazy, I know, but there it is. And we double date a lot. There's not the whole truth, but some, in that old chestnut about safety in numbers. That's why, last night, I—"

He stopped, but not soon enough. Jean stared at him, then she giggled. "Bill Chelton, don't tell me that you wanted us to go to the drive-in with you, last night, so that you could chaperone us?"

He fidgeted. "Well, I—"

She was off in a swirl of laughter. "Bill, this is wonderful! You thought you were—going to—save me—from a fate worse than death. You really did!"

"No, not quite. I just—well, darn it, Jean, I didn't want my sister going out with a guy who might make passes."

"You thought Andy would?"

"I didn't know. But when a guy's gone with a girl like Georgia for a couple of years, how's he going to know that all girls aren't the same?"

"Bill, you've forgotten one very important thing. You've forgotten *me*. Do I really look like the kind of girl who would—oh, honestly, I know you think I'm a kid, but I wasn't born yesterday. I know about—well, sex. Mom gave me the same books to read that she gave you. And girls talk about things, just the way boys do. I'll tell you something else. A lot of times parents—" smiling, she added, "and older brothers—worry about the wrong people. The ones they think are the nicest turn out to be the hellers and vice versa. I promise you, you don't have to worry about Andy. He's not the type. He's more interested in broken-down old cars than anything. But I hope I can make him interested in me. As for passes, he's made nary a one. Why, do you know, I had to kiss *him?*"

"You *what?*"

"I knew that would shock you. Stop looking so affronted. I wanted to, and I did, but I don't make a habit of it, honestly. So stop your worrying. And please try to act more human the next time Andy comes around. Once you know him, you'll like him."

"You sound very sure."

"Why shouldn't I be? We aren't talking about just anyone, we're talking about Andy Decker."

Bill chuckled. "I'm beginning to get it. Okay, Jean, you win. I'll learn to love the boy if I have to. But you'd better be right about him, or I'll—"

"You'll what?"

"I'll beat the living stuffing out of him. And out of you, too!"

Jean jumped off her perch. "My, my! Aren't we being big, brave, and noble tonight, though?" She pulled his ear as she passed, and got, in return, a good, hard spank on the bottom.

AUGUST

CHAPTER SIX

It couldn't be the second week in August, Jean thought. But it was. The small calendar on her desk, the one that had the words MARVIN JACOBSON, INSURANCE, printed across the bottom, told her that it was. The heavy, hot air outside her window told her that it was, as did the leaves on the trees which, though still green, were laden with late summer dust. The newspapers told her that it was, for half the ads proclaimed an August sale of furs, or white goods, or outdoor furniture, or swimming suits.

Some of the stores were featuring back-to-school clothes, and it seemed ridiculous to stop and finger a wool sheath while wearing white summer flats and a scoop-necked, sleeveless dress. It was much more appropriate to stop in somewhere for a drink, being careful to avoid those restaurants that featured French fries, for the smell of hot grease was unbearable on days like these. Tar oozed from sidewalk patches and clung stickily to shoes. The swimming pool at Launee was doing a record business, as was the drive-in.

No one hurried. Everyone sauntered. The summer was waning; it was on its last lap. There was nothing Jean could do, there was nothing anyone could do, to stop it. Not that Jean wanted time to come to a complete halt, but she wished it would slow down, so that all that she was experiencing could last just a little longer.

She was dating Andy, and her whole life was enclosed in this one throbbing fact. Mornings, while vacuuming the rugs, the thought of him caused her to cease moving the cleaner and to stand staring into space, completely oblivious to the whirring noise of the implement she was using. Often, when washing the dishes, she dropped a cup, or a glass, to the floor, and went about the business of sweeping the shattered particles without any awareness that something unusual had happened. Afternoons, while lying in the yard, or beside the Launee pool, the memory of something Andy had said the previous night was as warm as the sun beating down on her back.

She had dated him nine times since that night in mid-July when they'd gone to Roddy's and though her memory of other nights was vague, she forgot no detail of these particular times. She remembered with exactness the beige-checked shirt he had worn on the twenty-ninth of July, the pale green cotton she had worn, the way they had laughed over Mrs. Cunningham's German shepherd having a face exactly like Mrs. Cunningham. She remembered the shine of Andy's car (he'd spent two solid hours in polishing), the staleness of the popcorn they'd bought at the drive-in, the rain that had started halfway through the

38

movie, the leak in the roof of the car, and the malfunctioning of the windshield wipers. She remembered the sound of the fire siren that had blown in the middle of a lazy, August Sunday afternoon, Andy's immediate "let's go" response, their awed fascination as they watched one brick wall of Bolton's Bowling Alleys topple, and afterward, Mrs. Chelton's lecture regarding the dangers of dashing off to watch fires.

She remembered everything that had to do with Andy, but she forgot her appointment with the dentist, she forgot to return a library book, she forgot to buy a loaf of bread on her way home from the pool, she forgot to iron her white dress and it lay, dampened, in the laundry basket until it mildewed and had to be rewashed.

Before Andy there had been other boys. She had dated them two or three times, or six or seven, and when, by mutual consent, or mutual gravitation to someone else, they'd stopped, she'd remained friends with them. But she'd never felt about any of these boys the way she felt about Andy. She didn't know why; it was just so.

In the beginning, after her talk with Bill, she'd had doubts. She'd been more uncertain than she'd allowed Bill to know. She was no Victorian, but the thought of Andy parked with Georgia on Breck Hill was unsettling, the thought of Andy kissing Georgia was almost unbearable. Oh, forget it, she told herself over and over. You know darned well that a boy wouldn't go steady with a girl for two years without kissing her, for heaven's sake! As for anything else (in her thoughts she became vague at this point) most kids are a whole lot better than they're given credit for being.

She didn't admit, even to herself, exactly how upset she'd been, until after her next date with Andy. Because then she knew. Andy was—Andy. Straightforward, at times awkward, on occasion a bit shy. Hard-working, interested in cars, in people, in hot-rod magazines, science fiction, and, surprisingly, the works of Edgar Allan Poe. He couldn't swim very well, he danced just passably, he'd never had time for tennis, he thought walking was a waste of time except on hunting trips, he'd been just an average student. What, then, made him so appealing? Jean wasn't sure. All she knew was that she'd rather be with him than

39

with anyone she'd ever known. We just click, she might have said.

The days had whirled by. July had become history, and now half of August. Last night there had been a moon. Jean had sat on her own back porch, alone, because Andy had had to work late, and had wondered why writers of both poetry and prose always thought June, and perhaps October, were the only months worthy of moon mention. Surely no moon had ever compared with the splendor of the August one seen last night. Tonight it would be shining again and she was glad, for tonight she had a date with Andy.

"Hi, Jean," he said, as she opened the door to him. And, to Jean's father, "Hello, sir. I understand the Pirates got another one yesterday. I guess they've finally got their pitching problems solved."

"That's my team," Mr. Chelton said. "These Buccos are going to take the series, this year, you wait and see."

"I hope so. Hello, there, Betty, how's Floppy tonight?"

Betty giggled and stroked the ear of her inanimate, but constant, companion. "He's losing weight."

"You ought to get your big sister to feed him more. A little sawdust, say, or does he prefer foam rubber?"

How nice he is with her, Jean thought. She looks at him as though he were a combination of Santa Claus and that new singing cowboy. That her parents liked Andy, too, was becoming obvious from the naturalness with which they treated him. Even Bill, since that first time, had treated Andy with more friendliness, although Jean suspected that he still had mental reservations. Bill wasn't around much, though. He worked every day and was off some place with Maggie Phillipson every night.

"We've got to walk," Andy said. "My car seems to lose its innards as fast as Floppy, here. If we want to catch the last showing of the feature, we'd better get going."

"I've suddenly changed my mind," Jean said, "about wearing heels. Wait just a minute." She left the room.

Andy exchanged smiles with Mr. Chelton. "Why women wear 'em in the first place is a mystery to me," Mr. Chelton said.

"To me, too," Andy said. "Now that," as Jean appeared wearing flats, "is what the well-dressed girl

40

should always wear for a Saturday night movie date. It saves her escort from getting down on his hands and knees and hunting in the dark of a theater for a pair of missing shoes she couldn't stand one minute longer."

Jean laughed. "I know. Once, I lost a pair and they turned up three rows ahead of me. I thought, for a while, I would have to go home barefoot."

"That shouldn't be hard, for a hillbilly like you."

"That's enough, Decker."

"Yes, *ma'am,* Chelton. Let's go."

There was, to Jean, something satisfying in walking the familiar streets with Andy. She spoke self-consciously, but with a feeling of pride, to such neighbors as were visible, and she imagined them saying, "I see the Chelton girl's got a new boy friend. My, they make a nice-looking couple, don't they? I wonder who he is."

Down Harriott to Spring, turn right and continue to Center, then down Center to Seneca, and stroll past the shops before coming to the Drake Theater. Wave to the carload of kids that go past, stop and chat for a few minutes with Leroy Arnst, who emerges from Isaly's just as they pass, and somewhat sheepishly explains that the triple-decker cones he is carrying have been bought at the insistence of his kid brother, waiting now in a car by the bank.

Continue the saunter past Best's Jewelers and Hewitt's Shoe Store, Woolworth's and Mogilowitz's. Feel the heat radiating from the sidewalks with the intensity of an actual blast furnace. Listen to automobile horns, voices, occasional music; watch the changing of traffic signals and the time on the corner clock. Know, with deep conviction, that all these things are not ordinary, but will become a part of you forever because of the boy who is sharing them.

The theater was only partially filled, and they sat on aisle seats in the center section. Three rows ahead of them a man was sleeping. From two rows in back came an occasional "Sh! Be quiet now or we'll leave," which was addressed by a fat woman to a squirming little boy who kept wanting, in successive order, a drink, an end to the picture, a bag of popcorn, or to go to the bathroom.

Near the back some of the younger couples were necking, and Jean was very glad that Andy didn't put his arm around her, for she had always thought the way some kids huddled in the movies was rather disgusting. She wished, though, after a time, that he would hold her hand, but when it became apparent that he wasn't going to, she decided she might as well start to concentrate on the movie. So conscious of Andy had she been that she'd lost the thread of the story and never did manage to get more than a glimmer of what it was all about. She kept thinking that it must be good to absorb him so completely. He didn't glance at her at all, though she sneaked sidewise looks at him often. He didn't say anything, either, and an hour later she had the sudden, enervating thought that he was bored with her. He didn't really like her. He'd lost interest. This was the last time she would ever be with him.

The movie was over, at last. They walked home. Jean was quiet and so was Andy. What had happened? They had started out so joyously, and everything had gone so flat! Try as she might, Jean could think of nothing to say.

Then they were home and the house was dark. They would say good night, and would that be all? Forever?

"Well—" Did she dare ask him what was wrong?

Andy stood at the foot of the steps with her, and his hands were shoved into his pockets in a typical Andy gesture. He wasn't looking at her, but was staring at the street light halfway down the block. "Jean," he said. "Do you have to go right in?"

"No."

"Could we sit on the porch?"

"Of course." At least it wasn't going to end immediately.

They sat on the top step and Andy leaned his back against the porch pillar and clasped his hands around his knees. There were other people on other porches, and someone within the block was apparently listening to still another ball game, for Jean could hear the voice of the sportscaster saying, "And so we go into the bottom half of the fourth with a score of nothing—nothing." There was another sound that she couldn't at first identify, but then she discovered that it was the lawn sprinkler next door. Her neighbors had forgotten to turn it off.

Jean waited for Andy to speak. Any minute now he

42

would say, "Jean, this has been fun, but—" She waited and waited but he seemed in no mood to begin. She said, finally, "A penny?"

Now he looked at her. "Not for sale." Then, sitting straight, and smiling, he said, "But for a certain person they might be free."

The smile jolted her. It didn't fit with what she was sure he'd been thinking. She smoothed the blue dress she'd selected with such care. "How does one quality as a certain person?"

His smile deepened. She was glad that his soberness was disappearing for he began to look more like the Andy she knew. "Well," he said, "I guess, in the first place, one would have to be a girl."

"Like me?"

"Maybe. The one I've got in mind has got to look like a girl and act like a girl and *be* like a girl. She can't have any of these crazy, chopped off hairdos, you understand. She's got to have hair that's soft and it's got to curl a little when it's wet. She can't run around in shorts and slacks all the time, either. She's got to wear a dress once in a while, preferably blue. And she's got to act as though she has a little sense and not giggle all the time. She's got to have sort of dark eyes that don't flirt. She's got to be named Jean Chelton."

"Never, never had she felt such a whirling inner happiness. It was all right. *Everything* was all right. "Why, isn't that strange?" she asked softly. "*My* name is Jean Chelton."

"It is?" He tilted his head. "I do believe you measure up to the other qualifications, too. But there's one more. A darned important one. It's so important that I've been worrying about it all evening. All through the movie I kept trying to figure how I could find out, but I guess there's no way unless you tell me yourself."

"What do you want to know, Andy?"

"This girl," he said. "This one I've been talking about. What I want to know is whether she likes me. Enough to—as much as—" He leaned forward, and his voice became very serious. "As much as I like her. Do you, Jean?"

She didn't pretend. She was as serious as he. "I do like

43

you. Very much. We've only been dating for four weeks, Andy, but I like you better than any boy I've ever known."

"Then, what I've been trying to get up my courage to say is—Jean, will you wear this?" He was sliding the onyx ring off his finger; he was holding it toward her.

She took the ring. It was still warm from his wearing and quickly she slipped it over the third finger of her left hand. It was too large, but it was beautiful. It was Andy's.

The swirling within stopped; the happiness now was too deep for motion. She thought: Another boy might have put this ring on my finger. Another boy might have chosen a different setting. No one but Andy Decker would *hand* the ring to me, no one but Andy Decker would choose as his setting the front porch steps, where the only background music is that of a lawn sprinkler, plus the voice of an unseen sportscaster telling us that the baseball game has now reached the fifth inning. And yet, never again do I expect to feel the way I do right now. So hushed, and yet so alive. What can I say to him? Oh, how can I put into words all that I'm feeling? "Andy," she began, but that was as far as she got, for Andy Decker was kissing her.

Words were no longer necessary.

CHAPTER SEVEN

It wasn't until she was in her bedroom, winding thread over and over the ring, that Jean thought: I'm not the first girl to wear this. Did Georgia, too, have the same problem in making it fit?

She wished the thought had not occurred to her. It rubbed some of the luster from her happiness. The ring itself showed dullness on the band, and here, on the onyx, was a slight scratch. Had it been put there by Andy? Or by someone else?

She felt, suddenly, cheated. She wanted, more than anything, to be the first, the only girl in Andy's life. But she wasn't. She was second. Oh, forget it, Chelton, she told herself. Just because this is the first time for you, don't expect it to be—

To be what? There was enough thread on the ring now; she could apply colorless nail polish to finish the job of resizing. She dipped the brush and swabbed carefully. To be perfect? This wasn't an engagement ring, for heaven's sake, although her mother would probably act as though it were. Her mother wasn't going to like this. Her mother didn't believe in high school kids going steady. But, Jean thought, she'll have to change her thinking. She'll just have to. It's up to me to convince her.

Conversion, she discovered, was a difficult task. Her mother made no mention of the ring the next morning, nor did Jean, although she was sure her mother had noticed it while they were dressing for church. After dinner was over, Mr. Chelton said he guessed he'd take a "fiver," which meant that he would be napping for not five minutes but fifty. Bill announced that he was going over to the Phillipsons', and Betty gathered together the colored comic sheets of the Sunday paper. "I'm taking these down to Martha's," she said, "so's we can exchange."

"Jean," Mrs. Chelton said. "It's so hot. What do you say to trying the lilac?"

"All right, Mother," Jean said. Here it comes, she thought, and she wasn't mistaken.

"You know, of course," Mrs. Chelton said when they were settled in deck chairs, "that I want to talk to you."

"Yes."

"I'm sure you also know why."

Jean extended her hand. The onyx loomed large on her finger. It *felt* large, and bulky, and heavy. "This?"

Mrs. Chelton nodded. "Yes. It's Andy's, isn't it?"

"That's right. He gave it to me last night."

Mrs. Chelton sighed. "That's what I thought. Am I also right in thinking that this means you and Andy are going steady?"

Jean couldn't keep the lilt from her voice. "Yes, Mom, it does. But listen, Mom, listen—"

"I'm listening."

"Mom, I know how you feel about kids going steady.

45

But, honestly, you just don't understand how it is nowadays. It isn't like it was in olden times."

"No? Then suppose you set me straight. How do customs today vary from those of—" Mrs. Chelton smiled a little—"olden times?"

"Well," Jean said with great seriousness, "according to what I've heard you say, yourself, in *your* day the only kids that went steady were those that were going to get married. But today going steady doesn't mean that, at all. I mean, kids go steady with one person for a while, and then they go steady with someone else."

"Then what is the point? Why limit yourselves, if there's no serious purpose behind it?"

"Because—well, because that's the way things are done. Really, Mother, anybody who *is* anybody goes steady. I never have, before, because I was afraid you'd have a—I mean, I knew you wouldn't like it, and so I—but now I'm sixteen, and anyway, this time it's different. This time, don't you see, it's Andy?"

"Why does Andy make this time different from any other?"

She had admitted more than she realized. "Because I—well, because I like him."

"That's what I thought. I like him too. And I *do* understand how important it is to follow tribal custom. But I can't help wishing that this particular one had never got started. I don't know quite how or when it did, but I think I might have an idea as to why. I remember how things were with me, and I believe that one of the most important reasons, for a girl, in going steady, is security. It's nice to be sure of a date for the prom, or the basketball game, or the beach party, isn't it?"

"Yes," Jean said, "it is." She was inwardly amazed that her mother understood this all-important fact.

"But—" Her mother went on. "What happens to all this lovely security when couples break up? You just told me that kids go steady with one person for a while and then they go steady with someone else. What happens in the interim? What happens if the prom, say, comes along, between times? Between steadies, so to speak?"

"Well—" Jean said. "Well—" She felt helpless. "A girl just—just hopes, I guess."

46

"Exactly. Just as we used to hope in the old days. Which rather puts a snag in the smoothness of the security argument, doesn't it?"

"Yes, I suppose so."

"Do you know what I think, Jean? I think that the truth is that none of you youngsters is ready for that kind of security. You're too young, too inexperienced in judging people to know what you want. Real security in human relationships takes time in building, and it's based on love and understanding and respect. Security doesn't come about in a day, or a week, or even a few months. And, don't you see, dear, you've got to know a lot of people, all kinds of people, really, before you can decide on one particular person as being *the* one? And after you've decided, you've got to *work* for the security?"

"Just because I want to go steady with Andy doesn't mean that I think he's—" Jean began, and stopped. "That is, I do like him better than anyone else, but—"

"There! You see? You're not really sure."

But I am, Jean thought. I'm sure because Andy is Andy. He's not Leroy, or Jerry, or Jim, or any of the others I've dated. He's *Andy*. But I can't tell Mother that. She just doesn't *know*. "Maybe not," she said. "But, honestly, Mother, there's nothing *wrong* in wearing a boy's ring, is there?"

"No, there's nothing wrong in wearing a boy's ring. Jean, it's not the ring, but what it implies. It's the *segregation* that accompanies it—the isolation, that is wrong. The whole concept of today's generation on going steady is wrong. So many times boys and girls drop out of group activities that are necessary for wholesome development. I'm not alone in thinking this, either. At the last P.T.A. meeting—"

"Oh, the P.T.A.!" Jean interrupted, and her tone of voice suggested that anything said at a meeting of the P.T.A. could have no possible relation to the life of Jean Chelton.

"I know what you're thinking," her mother said. "But this subject of going steady was discussed very freely. Our speaker referred to it as a 'pretend marriage.' "

"A pretend marriage! What a ridiculous idea!"

"Is it? I'm inclined to think that the truth of such a term

47

is more obvious than the humor. Oh, I grant you that when young people start going steady, many times, it doesn't mean anything more than the security we were just talking about. It's not a matter of concern in the beginning. But later on, I'm not so sure."

"I don't see why."

"That's just it. You *don't* see. None of you think any farther than the moment. You don't understand the emotional involvement that may develop."

First Bill. Now her mother. Did they think she didn't know *anything?* "Mother, if you're trying to tell me—Mother, I know what happens to kids sometimes. Listen, is—how did you say it, emotional involvement? Is that your chief objection to going steady?"

"It's the chief objection of all parents," her mother said, "if they're thinking parents."

"Then stop thinking. You haven't got a thing to worry about. You trust me, don't you?"

"You know I do. I also, in this particular case, trust Andy. But human emotions, darling, cannot always be trusted. I want you to be aware of this, because I'm *not* going to forbid your going steady."

Jean was astonished. "You're *not?* Then, why—? I thought all this was intended—"

"All this was intended to help *you* think, and to get a few facts straight in your mind," Mrs .Chelton said. "If a mother doesn't talk these things over with her daughter, who is going to do it?"

Her brother, Jean thought. "You know, Mom, you are just wonderful. I honestly thought you were going to say, 'Absolutely no!' How come you didn't, feeling the way you do?"

Mrs. Chelton's answer was surprising. "Because you didn't hide Andy's ring, dear. Honesty like that is pretty wonderful in itself. The least I can do is respect it, and make an effort to go along with the times."

"You," Jean said, "are a mother to set an example for all mothers." She meant it. And she thought suddenly of Genevra Coffman, who was going steady with Tom Maheney, but whose mother didn't know it. She smiled. "Then it's all right? I won't have to meet Andy at Virginia's house, or at Grandy's, or the library?"

"Andy will come here," Mrs. Chelton said. "If he and my daughter are going to go steady, I want to know him a whole lot better."

"What did your parents say?" Andy asked her that night. "About this?" He touched the ring, and then, very naturally, his fingers closed around hers.

"Now how," Jean asked, "do you expect me to eat cake when you're hanging on to me? Are you trying to keep me from getting fat?"

They were sitting at the breakfast bar in the Chelton kitchen and they were alone. Earlier, they'd watched a series of television programs with Jean's parents and Betty. But after the eleven o'clock news, the other Cheltons had retired. "Don't get caught in the late movie, children," Mrs. Chelton had said.

"We won't," Jean had promised. "We're going to fix something to eat, and then Andy's leaving. Aren't you, Andy?"

"Yup!" Andy had said, and everyone had laughed at his imitation of the Western marshal they'd been watching. He said it again now, and added, "Forget the cake, Chelton. Come on, tell me."

"Oh," Jean said casually, "they wanted to know if your intentions are honorable."

"They *what?*" He dropped her hand and made a declamatory gesture with his own. "The Little Nell bit, huh? Never darken our doorstep again!"

Jean giggled. "Yup! And 'shoot if you must this old gray head.'"

"Careful, Chelton, you're mixing the scripts!"

They both laughed, and Andy swigged milk from the brown stoneware mug. He wiped his lips, desperado fashion, with the back of his hand. "Wa'al, seein' as how the mortgage is due—Jean Chelton, what *did* your parents say? Seriously?"

"Nothing much. Mother is the only one who knows, as yet, but it's all right with her. And anything that's all right with her is all right with Dad."

"So!" Again Andy held her hand, but this time the ring was visible, and both of them looked at it. "It's all legal. You're really my girl."

The way he said it and the way he looked at her caused an effervescence within Jean. "Yes," she said quietly, and was surprised that the fizzing didn't show in her voice. "I guess I am."

"You *guess?* You've got to do better than that. Maybe this will convince you." His counter stool tilted on two legs, necessitating a short kiss. But though it was short, it was as sweet as the chocolate cake lying forgotten on the yellow counter. "Now do you know?"

"I'm still not sure." Then, as he leaned toward her, his eyes mischievous, she sobered. "I was just teasing. But, you see, I've never been anyone's girl before."

"I know."

"You know?" She was perturbed. It wasn't exactly complimentary to be known as a girl who had never had a boy friend. Oh, dates, of course, but never anyone special. "How did you know that?"

"Guys always know. Girls who've been out a lot have certain ways about them. But it isn't only that. About *you* I wanted to learn. And so I did. You might be surprised if you knew how much."

"For instance?"

"You want a catalogue? Okay, you'll get it. I know that when you go to the library you head straight for the rental section and look over all the new books before you disappear behind the reference section. I know that you leave for school about eight-twenty in the morning, and that you always order a Pepsi in Grandy's, and that you and Virginia Montrie are like *that.*" He made a two-fingered gesture. "I know that you took your driver education this last spring under Mr. Houseman, and that your favorite subject is Physics, but that you hate World History. I know that you go fishing with your father and your brother and that you're a darned good swimmer. I *ought* to know that! I know that your hair falls over your eyes, sometimes, and that you always chew on your pencil when you're taking a test. I know—"

"You know too much," Jean interrupted. "You're a regular private eye. Are none of my secrets safe?"

"I hope not. I want to know *all* about you. Everything. What brand of toothpaste you use, and how you feel about me, and whether you can recognize the makes of various cars, and do you think boys who carry umbrellas look screwy, and how you feel about me, and do you like to get up in the morning, and how you feel about me, and do you think girls ought to wear slacks, and do you, too, loathe liver, and how do you feel about me?"

"Andy, you're impossible!"

"Okay, I get the message. You can't stand the sight of me." He got off the stool and headed for the back door. "But don't disillusion me further. Please, I beg of you, if you like liver, spare me the information."

"I hate it."

He grinned. "Good girl. See you tomorrow night?"

"Wait a minute, Andy."

He came back. "That's right. I *am* forgetting something." He leaned toward her.

"No," she said. "That isn't what—no, I didn't mean—I just wanted to tell you—"

He waited. "Yes?"

"Decker, go home. I can't remember. You confuse me."

"I'm going." He made a kissing motion with his lips, but he didn't touch her. "Good night, angel."

When he had gone Jean, stepped out on the porch. She looked with proprietary interest at the golden circle in the sky. This moon was hers, as was this night, and this ring on her finger. Suddenly, for no particular reason, she wanted to feel the grass on her bare feet. She kicked off her shoes, tiptoed down the steps, and walked slowly, with glorious sensuality, on the dew-swept lawn. How cool it felt! How exactly as she'd thought! So sort of squishily pleasant! And the cicadas! Wasn't their chirping marvelous when everywhere else was utter stillness? As for the scents—the late summer flowers, even at night, could create perfumes. Jean stretched her arms toward the sky. This belongs to me, she thought. Oh, *Andy!*

She was going steady with Andy Decker. She was his girl. And she hoped that tomorrow, when she went swimming at Launee, the pool would be crowded. She wanted as many people as possible to know that she was wearing his ring.

CHAPTER EIGHT

The blue-painted pools at Launee were not crowded; neither the shallow one intended for wading, nor its deeper counterpart. A few youngsters clambered about the constantly playing fountain in the center of the smaller pool, and in the larger, perhaps half a dozen people were crawl-stroking, or breast-stroking, or diving, depending upon their various abilities. But everywhere along the concrete strips at the edge of the pools, and on the grass which reached to the enclosing fence, partly clad humanity was visible.

The girls who waited on customers at the refreshment stand doled out pop and candy bars and potato chips and ice cream bars and pretzels. They wiped sweat from their faces and counted change and said, "Oh, yeah? Sure you're kidding?" and "No, there's no deposit on the bottles if you leave 'em."

High in the lifeguard stand, wearing dark trunks and the inevitable white sailor hat, a lifeguard leaned back under the canopy and indolently eyed the girls who were forever coming to ask him what was the temperature of the water, or did he want something to drink, or did he ever go to the dances at the Y? At times he would get to his feet, blow the whistle that was attached to a chain around his neck, frown, and wave a struggling swimmer toward the shallow end of the pool. But for the most part he would just sit, surveying his domain, and wishing that some of the really sharp girls, the smooth good-looking kids, would come around and talk to him. But they never did. He was stuck with the fat ones, the bow-legged ones, the silly ones who giggled everlastingly.

Jean Chelton and Virginia Montrie emerged from the dressing rooms, carrying necessary accoutrements. The nails on their toes flashed brightly vermilion as they made their way directly to the strip at the deep end of the pool.

Their fingernails, however, as they spread beach towels and checked on equipment, showed no signs of polish. Virginia's towel was gaily imprinted with fish, Jean's with sailing boats. Not for them the kind that read BEWARE! or HANDS OFF! Too obvious, they'd decided several years ago.

"Have we got everything?" Jean asked. "Let's see, baby oil, iodine, sun glasses, radio, lipstick."

"Comb, pencil, change, deck of cards," Virginia inventoried. "I guess we're all set."

They sat on the beach towels and applied oil to their legs and arms. Finished, they rubbed oil into each other's backs. Then, the ritual completed, they began to look around, checking on who was there.

"I see Liz and Leroy," Virginia said.

"Where?"

"Back by the fence. Honestly, the way they act in public is just sickening."

"I know. Somebody ought to tell them. Oh, look, Marge has got a new bathing suit. I wish I had the figure to wear one like that."

"If you had, I hope you wouldn't show it the way she does."

"Cat."

"Well, it's the truth! Oh, hello, Gee, how's the water?"

"I wouldn't know," the girl who was passing said. "I haven't tried it yet. Hey, Tommy, wait up! I want a frozen sucker!"

"They're becoming quite a thing, aren't they?" Jean said. "Genevra and Tommy, I mean. How does she get away with it?"

"Oh, you know. Meet at the corner stuff. One of these days, Mrs. Coffman's going to catch 'em at one of the dances, or she's going to learn that Genevra isn't really spending the evening with a girl friend, and when she *does*—powie! All hell will break loose."

"I know. I feel sorry for them. They're good kids, but Mrs. C. is so darned strict!"

"Well," Virginia said, "at least *you* don't have that problem. Let me see your ring again."

On the blanket next to them, a girl who had been lying on her stomach, rolled over and sat up. "Hi, Chelton. Hi,

Montrie. Hey, what's that you've got, Jean?"

"Hello, Marcia. What does it look like?"

"It looks like—well, what do you know? Is it Andy Decker's?"

"Yes."

Marcia poked a second girl, who was lying beside her. "Wake up, Mid. I've got something to tell you. You'll never guess who's wearing whose ring."

Mid sat up. "Oh, hi! One of you guys? Oh, you, Jean. Well, congratulations. And good luck." She lay down again, but a moment later she got up. "How about walking over to the refreshment stand, Marcia? I'm dying of thirst."

"And that's not all she's dying of," Virginia said, when the other two had left. "Watch her! She can hardly wait to tell everyone. Do you mind?"

"No," Jean said. "I *want* everyone to know."

"But—" Virginia said. She hugged her knees, and gazed thoughtfully at the water. She was a thin girl, whose face would show real beauty if it ever filled out, and her hair was the envy of all the girls at senior high. It just missed being gold, and it fell softly to her shoulder. At times she put it on the top of her head, and today she had caught it back in a pony tail, so that the fine modeling of her face seemed more pronounced. "It might not work out. It might not last. And then how will you feel?"

"But it will," Jean said.

"You don't know that. It didn't last with Georgia."

"I wish people would forget about Georgia," Jean said. "Honestly, every other minute, someone keeps reminding me. Can't I just be happy without having to remember her all the time?"

"She's back in town," Virginia said. "You won't be able to forget. How are you going to feel when you see her?"

"Just the way I always do."

"No," Virginia said. "You won't. You're going to feel a little embarrassed, and I'll bet my best bottle of Intimate that you'll wait to see if she speaks first."

That's probably, Jean thought, exactly what I'll do, and the way Virginia knows these things is positively uncanny. "Time will tell," she said lightly.

"You are so right. Time will tell a lot of things. Jean,

54

maybe I shouldn't say this, but I can't help wondering—oh, forget it. I'm going to shut my big mouth."

"No, go ahead. You started to say something; you might as well finish."

"You won't like it."

"I promise not to get mad."

"All right. When Andy and Georgia broke up, who did the ditching?"

"Oh, it was just mutual, I think." She knew better. Andy himself had told her that Georgia was the one to take the initiative. But he'd also told her that he'd tried earlier. So she wasn't really lying

Virginia smiled. "That's good. That takes the point out of what I was going to say."

"Which was?"

"I was afraid Andy might be—well, you know—*showing* Georgia."

"Why should he do that?"

"Well, if Georgia *had* ditched him, and since, as I hear it, she's already going steady again, the possibility exists that he might have dated you just to prove he didn't care."

"He could have, I guess, but I don't think so." Not for anything would she admit to Virginia that the possibility had also occurred to her. She decided to change the subject. "Are you going in?"

"Yes, for a few minutes."

"Come on, then, let's go."

They strolled self-consciously to the diving board, posed prettily for a few seconds, then each in turn ran three quick steps to the end of the board and dove. They were excellent swimmers and they knew they were being watched. They didn't mind observation as long as they were in the water. It was the trek from and back to the beach towels that undermined morale and caused them to pull their suits down over their thighs, adjust straps, straighten shoulders, hold stomachs rigidly in.

The beach towels, when they got back to them, were havens of security. Once again they went through the ritual of oiling their bodies.

"Want to play some gin?" Virginia asked.

"As soon as I pin up my hair. If I don't, it will just hang tonight." Jean bobby-pinned her hair quickly and expertly and tied a scarf around it. She donned sun glasses. "Ready."

The afternoon waned. They talked and played cards and lay at times on their stomachs, at times on their backs, with arms folded across their eyes. The sun beat down on them, warming them, filling them with indolence. "Well," Jean said, at last, "if I'm to get ready for my date tonight—" She rose and stretched. Virginia removed her sun glasses and packed away paraphernalia. They were all talked out and in silence they left the pool.

"How was the swimming?" Mrs. Chelton asked, when Jean walked into the kitchen and flung her beach bag on top of the dryer.

"Absolutely wonderful!" Jean said, and her answer did not strike her as being at all incongruous for a person who had been in the water a mere five minutes.

SEPTEMBER

CHAPTER NINE

The summer was almost over. With the first days of September there came a change. The sun seemed as hot as ever, yet everyone knew that it was gradually putting more distance between itself and the earth. There was a lessening of the crowds on the beaches, and the bathing suits, so vivid at the start of the season, were sun and water faded. There were fewer out-of-state licenses on passing cars, fewer customers at the ice cream drive-ins, fewer fishermen along the river banks.

Driving on the highways, one became conscious of the farmers working in their fields, making preparation for fall. Fruit stands along the way featured ripe, red home-grown tomatoes, purple plums, green cucumbers for pickling.

In town, an occasional dark transition cotton stood out among the pastel dresses and the shorts that most girls were still wearing. Sweaters and light jackets were seen in the evenings.

People no longer talked of the weather, nor of where they planned to spend their vacations. They talked of what teams would play in the World Series, of the opening of school, of the initial fall meetings of various clubs, of how things looked for this year's football team.

It had been, Jean thought, the most wonderful summer of her life. She had wanted it to last, but now that it was nearly over she discovered that she was looking forward to fall and winter. This would be her final year in high school. To be a senior was in itself a kind of an award for accomplishment. To be a senior and to be going steady with Andy Decker was to have all of life's finest at one and the same time. What was summer, after all, but a few short months? This was to be her year!

Day after tomorrow she and Andy would walk through the entrance doors at the high school together. Already he'd told her that he planned to come by for her and that she'd better be ready. "I never," he'd said, "have more than the exact number of minutes needed to make it."

"I'll be ready," Jean had promised. She'd thought: It will all be so perfect.

Bill didn't agree with her. He hadn't liked the idea of her going steady. "It will make a difference in the year that ought to be your best," he'd said.

"It's the difference, Bill, that will make it the best," she'd told him. "I've never gone steady before, and I'm glad I waited until I was a senior. It's the à la mode on the pie, don't you see?"

"I see that you're a very determined young lady. I still think it's a mistake."

"Why? Because the boy happens to be Andy? You don't like him, do you?"

Bill had hesitated. "I like him well enough. I don't really know him. Maybe he's got a little to do with the way I feel, but it isn't wholly that. I'd feel the same way about anyone because I don't think it's the smart thing to do. Maybe you didn't know this, Jean, but the trend, nowadays, is *away* from going steady, particularly in high school. It's not a big trend, as yet, but it's growing. Most of the fellows and girls I know say that if they had it to do over again they would never tie themselves down to one person."

"That sounds just fine," Jean had said. "In theory. You and your friends really have all the answers. I suppose the fact that you don't believe in going steady is the reason there are so many marriages in college."

"Sister, you surely know how to turn an argument to your favor."

"Were we arguing? I wasn't aware of it."

"There's a whole lot, Miss Chelton, that you aren't aware of."

"Says the big college man."

"Jean Chelton, I could throttle you. Oh, well, go ahead. Make your own mistakes, but don't say I didn't warn—"

"Don't be so pompous! I don't need warning. And you didn't either. There was a little girl named Mary-Elizabeth with whom you went steady in your junior year. And another one—Carol Downey, wasn't it—in your senior year? But you survived, didn't you?"

"Yes, I survived. Thank the Lord!"

"All right! All I ask, Bill Chelton, is that you live your life and let me live mine. Or is that asking too much?"

He'd come after her, then, with the broom, and she'd escaped to the porch. But the conversation had troubled her. She liked her brother, and had had, within recent years, real respect for his opinion. Until now. About this one thing he was wrong.

Now, two days before the start of the fall term, Jean sat in a cool, sudsy tub and thought of other times, other years, when she'd gone to school with Virginia and Susy and Liz. She remembered her first day at senior high when, as a tenth grader, she'd gone with nine other girls. They'd been so scared! And yet how quickly they'd fallen into the routine of high school life!

Within two weeks they were complaining of the cafeteria food and of the homework loaded on them by the science teacher. They knew which stairs were to be used for descent of classes, which for ascent, from fourth floor to the basement and back again. They no longer wandered into the principal's office by mistake; this was the room they now avoided whenever possible. They found their assigned seats in the auditorium as though they'd been using them for years, they spoke knowledgeably of the "shop" boys, the "chem" lab, of the way

Miss Polti checked on the second floor "lav," of "Doc" Andrews, who taught Biology, of "Muddy" Waters, who coached the J.V.'s. They reported to each other which senior boys had spoken to them in the halls, which teachers they liked, which they couldn't stand, which courses were tough, which were easy. Yes, on the surface, they'd adjusted, but all the time they'd known that, compared to the seniors, they were as nothing.

And now, those who had been seniors then were as nothing. They'd gone on to college, or to jobs. Some of them were married and already had children. Occasionally an item about one of them appeared in the local paper. John McCarthy makes the dean's list at the state university; Mr. and Mrs. Carrothers announce the engagement of their daughter Sara; Harry Summers, who is stationed at Lackland Air Force Base, has been promoted to the rank of corporal. And reading about John McCarthy, and Sara Carrothers, and Harry Summers, was like reading about chance acquaintances. These people had nothing to do with oneself. The important people, the people who mattered, were Virginia Montrie, and Tom Evans, and Leroy Arnst, and Liz Perkins, and Andy Decker, and Gee Coffman. This year's seniors!

Tonight thirty of them were having a beach party, as a kind of last fling to summer, or to undergraduate days, or even to being young. Because, of course, from now on, they would be mature. As seniors they might never again want to engage in anything so juvenile as a wiener roast. They would be participating in responsible and important and adult activities.

So, as she relaxed in the tub, Jean thought with nostalgia of days gone, but with anticipation of days to come. But she'd better stop thinking, she decided, regarding the water-soaked wrinkles on her hands. Andy would be here in ten minutes and—oh, heavens! Had Betty replaced the frankfurters she'd used for last night's cookout in Martha Johnson's yard?

Betty hadn't replaced them, but she'd only used two. "Will six be enough?" Jean asked, minutes later.

None of the other Cheltons were home. They were off on their own Labor Day picnic and though they would be returning shortly, they had not yet arrived.

Andy, who had come just after she'd made it to the kitchen, sat at the counter and watched her. "Sure," he said. "Two for you and four for me." He began to sing. "And we will raise a fam-il-ee—"

Jean giggled. 'Of hot dogs?"

"No. Quit spoiling my act!" He came around the counter and put his arms around her, pulling her close as he finished the song. "Oh, can't you see how happy we will be?"

She stood perfectly still. She had to because of this inward lurching. He was so close, and he smelled of clean clothes and antiseptic soap, and his green-brown eyes were smiling at her lazily, and there, right underneath the left eyebrow was a small white scar. She'd never noticed it before, but she wanted, suddenly, to touch it. "Andy," she said. "I—"

She hadn't meant to, but she dropped the frankfurters. "Oh, look!" Confused, she knelt to retrieve them. It seemed anticlimactic. Andy had been about to kiss her. She'd wanted him to. But here she was, gathering from the floor what they were supposed to eat later. "What'll we do?"

"Rinse 'em off," Andy said. "Here, give them to me."

If he'd intended to kiss her, he'd certainly lost the notion. Probably, Jean thought, he thinks I did it on purpose. Maybe it's just as well. For a minute I felt so odd, almost unreal. I wonder where he got that scar.

She didn't ask him. She packed the frankfurters, the buns, the mustard, a fat purple onion, in a wicker tote bag. "I'm ready."

"You'll need a jacket."

Her jacket was brown and wouldn't go with the green and black plaid of her slacks. Last year's black sweater, though old, would have to do, and she slung it over her arm.

Andy said, as he stowed the tote bag and plastic-lined beach bag in the car, "I got root beer for us, although some of the other guys will probably bring straight stuff. Will you mind?"

The idea of regular beer for a beach party was new to her. "No," she said. "That is, I don't—would you rather have had—I mean, will you feel that it's sissy not to?"

"Gosh, no. I'm driving, and I've got too much respect for traffic conditions to take any chances. Besides, I don't like it. I tried it once, and if you happen to like swamp water, I suppose it's okay. Why some of these guys go for it is something I'll never understand. I guess they figure it makes them big shots, but most of them, after one bottle, act darned silly."

They drove toward Lake Eileen, twenty miles away. They didn't make particularly good time, for the traffic was heavy. "Here we are," Jean said once, "just starting out, and everyone else is on the way home."

She was very happy. It had taken a lot of talking to get her parents' permission for this party. She hadn't been able to present the usual argument that all the kids were going. Virginia wasn't, nor Susy, although Liz Perkins would be there, and Gee Coffman. Still, these were the only two that she knew more than slightly. Even Andy didn't know all the kids too well, although the invitation had come from him. Someone, he'd said, had made the suggestion, a few others had taken it up, and altogether there would be about fifteen couples.

But it hadn't been the guest list that had worried her parents as much as the Labor Day traffic. "Any other day," her mother had said, "we wouldn't mind so much. But every year there are so many accidents."

"Andy's a careful driver," Jean had said. And she thought now: I'm glad he doesn't drink, but it's more than just the driving. I'd hate to have him go all sloppy.

Most of the others had preceded them to the beach. Darkness would soon be upon them, but now, while there was still grayness in the sky, they were scurrying about gathering driftwood for the fire they would build later. A few of the boys, even fewer of the girls, were already swimming, and Andy and Jean, after they had collected their share of firewood, decided to join them.

Jean stood behind Andy's car and stripped off the slacks and shirt that covered her swimming suit. She waited for Andy, who had gone back in the woods to change, but after a few minutes she felt conscious of her aloneness. Someone might think she was an extra girl or, worse, that her boy friend had deserted her. She ran to the water and, just as she plunged, saw a new car drive up. She couldn't be sure, at this distance, but she thought the girl who got out was Georgia Kane.

The lake was small and there were no breakers. Jean swam out beyond the kids who were laughing and screaming near shore. She turned on her back and floated, trying to organize her thoughts. Had it really been Georgia? No, of course not. This was a party for seniors. But was it? No one had actually said that it was. For all she knew there might be tenth graders in the crowd. Seniors didn't have to stick with seniors. Georgia hadn't, last year. She'd gone steady with a junior. She'd gone with Andy. Maybe, right now, she was standing on the beach talking to him, asking him how he'd been and if he remembered the time they'd—they'd what? There would be so many things for them to remember! And I, Jean thought, am jealous. I've always been jealous; I've never been quite sure that Andy could really prefer me to Georgia. Look at me now, lying in the water, and feeling scared and lost and out of things. I'll have to go back. I can't stay here indefintely. But if that girl is Georgia I don't know what I'll do.

The girl wasn't Georgia. Her name was Rosalie and she had Georgia's blonde hair and a close resemblance to Georgia's figure, but none of Georgia's smoothness. Her laughter was too loud, her slacks too tight fitting, and her wisecracks too knowing.

These things, Jean learned later, after they were sitting around the fire. In the meantime she had a more pressing problem, for Andy was miffed. "Listen," he said, as she emerged from the water, "when I take a girl to a beach party I expect her to *be* my girl, and not go dashing off into the lake where I can't find her. I felt like a fool, running around asking people if they'd seen you."

She stood before him, dripping. "I'm sorry."

"You ought to be."

"Well, I said I was. What more do you want?"

"What I don't want is sarcasm."

"I'm not the one who's being sarcastic."

"Oh, no?"

"Andy, please! I am sorry, but if you're going to act like a spoiled brat. I'll—"

"So now I'm a spoiled brat!"

"Andy, stop it! I don't intend to stand here and fight

with you. Let's go back in the water."

"Why? So you can complete the job of showing me up? No, thanks."

"Then I'm going to get dressed. You do whatever you want to, Mr. Andy Decker. It makes no difference to me." She took a backward step, but he caught her hand roughly. "Oh, no, you don't."

She broke away from him and ran toward the car. She was very close to tears and, in the darkness, she didn't see the rock until she stumbled against it and fell.

Someone was helping her to her feet. "Jean," Andy said, "I'm a louse. A big, fat, crackling louse. I ought to be stepped on." He pressed his cheek against hers. "Angel, you're not crying?"

"No. I've been swimming, remember?"

"I remember. You are, too, crying. Are you hurt?"

"No, I just—oh, Andy, please let's not fight! I truly didn't mean to make you mad when I went in the water without you."

"I believe you. I made a big issue out of nothing. And we won't fight, Angel." He added ungrammatically, but earnestly, "Never, nowhere, nohow, no more, and I hereby seal my promise." He kissed her, and she thought that his hands on her shoulders, felt warm. She wondered if it was because she was cool from the water, and she wondered if she'd have noticed it at all if she hadn't been in her bathing suit.

CHAPTER TEN

By the time Jean and Andy had changed ("I've got to get out of dry trunks into dry slacks," Andy had said) the others had a blazing fire going.

"Hi," Liz Perkins said, as they sat on a blanket beside her. "Where've *you* two been?"

"Around," Jean answered. She felt guilty. The crowd probably thought she and Andy had been off somewhere, necking. "I was in the water, and then I had to—"

"Don't bother explaining, doll," one of the boys said. "We know the score."

Jean disliked him immediately. His name, she knew, was something or other Garvey. She had seen him at school and had thought he looked like a wrestler.

"Shut up, Garve," Andy said. "The girl is telling the truth."

"Oh, sure, sure. I didn't mean anything; I'm a harmless critter. Ask Rosalie." He turned to the girl beside him, the one who, from a distance, had resembled Georgia Kane.

"Critter," Rosalie said, "I'll go along with. About harmless I'm not so sure, boy." Her voice had a scratchy, bawdy note.

Genevra Coffman leaned across Liz to whisper. "Where did he get her?"

Andy shrugged. "Search me."

"Bailey's Tavern, I think," Leroy said.

"She looks it," Liz said, and Genevra and Jean nodded.

Why did Garve have to bring her? Jean thought. She's certainly not a senior. She's never gone to our school. She looks three years older than the boys, even. I wish she weren't here.

Andy said, very low, "That Garvey ought to have his head examined. Don't pay any attention to what he said. He was just mouthing off."

"I won't."

She didn't, for a time. She talked and laughed and whispered with the group around her, and she thought: I'm glad Gee and Liz are here. If they weren't there'd be no one for us to sit with.

The group was divided into definite cliques. Garve and Rosalie and two other couples sat across from them, some distance back from the fire, in the shadows. Millicent Edwards and Janet Marshall and their crowd were ranged on a log at right angles to them. Sitting on blankets to the left were Mary Lawrence and Tip McGinty and Marg Evans and Jim Wooster, plus some couples whom Jean knew by sight only. There had been no introductions, nor were any forthcoming.

Mary Lawrence was the first to suggest some games. "Does anyone know a good one?"

"Sure," Garve called out. "I know a—"

He was ignored. Millicent Edwards jumped to her feet "How about questions and answers? You know, the game where somebody gives all the kids on this side the questions and somebody else gives the ones over there just any old answer and then we ask and answer out loud?"

"It's a good game," Tommy Maheney said. "Remember, Andy, we played it at one of—"

Genevra grabbed him. "Oh, heavens! Get that bug off me!" Then she whispered, "Shut up, Tommy!" and Jean overheard her.

Andy said, "Yeah, I remember the game."

They had played it at one of Georgia's parties. Of this Jean was sure. And it was sweet of everyone to try to protect her from the knowledge, but she didn't need protection. She moved slightly away from Andy but he didn't seem to notice.

The game was fun. Some of the answers didn't fit the questions at all, but when Janet Marshall said, "Where were you at three o'clock on the morning of June the fifth?" and Jim Wooster said, "Out in the middle of the lake with Miss Polti," everyone whooped and some of the boys literally rolled.

The atmosphere was friendlier after that. Shared laughter has a way of leveling differences in people. Now, even Rosalie was tolerated, although she was probably the only one who hadn't understood the joke.

Liz and Leroy started the singing and it lasted for an hour. Jean, listening to Andy's voice, smiled to herself. He knew the words, but she was sure he didn't suspect that he was seldom in tune.

The fire burned to coals and it was time to roast the frankfurters. They were charred and delicious. Beverages were lifted from portable refrigerators, bottle caps snapped, the volume controls on portable radios were tuned up and the dissonant sounds from three separate programs blared forth until someone said, "Let's synchronize."

Inevitably one of the boys took the cue and turned to the girl beside him. "That's what we do best, isn't it, sweetheart?"

"Oh, you!"

The moon rose and the fire, with added wood, burned on. The air became cool and a slight breeze caused a lap-slap sound on the lake that was infinitely lulling, infinitely satisfying. Laughter lessened; voices became lower and, in some cases, ceased altogether. Jean leaned back in the enclosing circle of Andy's arm and thought: This is a perfect way to end the summer.

It was Garve, of course, who marred the perfection. Garve and Rosalie and a few of the others had been drinking beer all evening. Jean had said nothing, nor had anyone else. It seemed to be understood that, in a crowd of this size, the majority could overlook the behavior of the minority. It was a *to each his own* philosophy that imparted a feeling of worldliness and superiority to those who shared it. Up to a point. The point where worldliness was shattered and tolerance disappeared came when Garve jumped to his feet and stood swaying in the firelight. "This party," he said thickly, "is dyin'. It needs a li'l life, an' I know jus' the babe who c'n give it to us. C'mon, Rosalie, doll, le's give the a—a—assembled multitude a li'l dance. What d'ya say?"

"Aw, sit down, Garve," Rosalie said. "I don't want to. Not now."

"Sure you do," Garve said. He looked at the circle of faces watching him and grinned, obviously pleased that he had secured attention. "This li'l girl is the greates' li'l dancer ever to hit this town. Wait'll you see her? C'mon, now, Rosie, make 'em sit up and take notice!" He leaned down and pulled Rosalie to her feet; lost his balance, but recovered.

Rosalie, Jean noted, seemed anxious. "I don't really think I ought to, Garve."

Garve looked ugly. "Lissen," he said, "if you don't, I'm goin' to report you to—"

"Okay." Rosalie twisted her hands together. "But I've got to have music."

Garve turned up the radio. "You've got it," he said. "Go to it, babe." And then he yelled the oldest words in the history of burlesque: "Take 'em off!"

Jean felt Andy's arm tighten suddenly. From her left she heard Tom Maheney's voice say, "Oh, Jeez, not that!"

Not what? She wondered, but in a few minutes she

66

knew. For Rosalie was dancing, and it was dancing that was unlike anything Jean had ever seen. There was a swaying of her hips in the tight-fitting slacks, a thrusting of the body that was purely carnal. The dance was cheap, and vulgar, and suggestive, and Jean felt as though she were being dragged through slime, mile after mile of it. Yet she watched. Everyone did. Garve, with a leer; a few of the boys sheepishly; the rest completely expressionless.

The music went on. The dance went on until Rosalie, looking anxious and glancing appealingly at Garve, unfastened the three top buttons of her shirt and danced back toward the woods, beyond vision.

No one moved. No one spoke.

"Well, c'mon, everybody," Garve said. "Where's the applause?"

There was none. Rosalie didn't reappear and Garve glared belligerently. "Well, what d'ya know? It's a damned Sunday school convention! Wait a minute, Rosie, we'll go where we're appreciated." He staggered away, and from the woods they heard the sound of a girl's crying, and Rosalie's scratchy voice saying, "I told you I didn't want to. I knew they wouldn't understand."

Mary Lawrence said quietly, "I think it must be awfully late. I hate to break this up, but I'm afraid I'll have to go." Her words might have been a motion; moved, seconded and passed unanimously, for everyone began to collect gear. No one looked directly at another person. No one had much to say. The boys carried water from the lake and doused the fire while the girls waited in the cars.

All Jean wanted was to go home and scrub and scrub. She couldn't talk, not even to Andy. She sat a foot away from him in the car, and she thought: If he tries to kiss me good night I can't bear it!

But Andy didn't. He said, once, "I didn't know about Garve, Jean." And later, when he walked with her to the door, he said, "I'm sorry."

"I'm sorry, too. Good night, Andy."

"Good night, Jean."

That was all. She was grateful to him because he left immediately.

Jean's manner, the next day, was subdued. This was in direct contrast to former years, when the day before the opening of the fall term of school had meant excited telephone conferences with friends as to what to wear, where to meet, and when. The decisions to be made had seemed important. Should she wear her hair up or down? And would white flats be all right, or were most of the kids planning on tennis shoes?

Today she could think of nothing but what had happened last night. True, the whole incident involving Garve and Rosie seemed not quite so shocking when viewed in retrospect, from the living room of her own home, with the sunlight pushing in under the partially lowered blinds. Still, she had only to close her eyes to experience again the unexpected shame she had felt, the guilt.

For the first time she had come up against crudeness. She'd been aware of differences in people; she'd bracketed Rosalie and Garve, too, as being the Bailey's Tavern type. But she hadn't really *known*. Well, now she did.

Oddly enough, remembering Rosalie's reluctance; remembering the sound of her crying, she felt a little sorry for the girl. It was Garve who had subjected all of them to something they'd rather not have seen. He was older than most; he was what the kids called a "two-for-one," meaning that many times it had taken him two years to complete a scheduled year of school work. Was it only stupid people who went in for that sort of thing? Or did smart ones, too? She hoped not, but how could she know?

She stood, dust cloth in hand, before the mahogany breakfront and read uncomprehendingly the titles of the books behind glass doors. *Lady of the Lake, The Case of the Missing Heiress, Marmion, Twenty Thousand Leagues Under the Sea, My Three Years with Eisenhower, Brave Men, The Man in the Gray Flannel Suit, The Holy Bible, Betsy and Joe, The Home Book of Sewing, Grimm's Fairy Tales, Celia Garth, A Child's History of Art.*

She picked up Betty's magic eight ball, once used so enthusiastically for telling fortunes, but now a paper weight. She dusted it carefully, then held it tightly in her hands, feeling, in some indefinable way, that from its hard surface she would gain reassurance.

Perhaps she did, for suddenly she attacked her dusting chores with more vigor, and it wasn't until she was doing the piano that inertia caught up with her again. She sat on the bench, and eventually her fingers found the keys and she began to play. She wasn't expert, but there was a piece called "Fingal's Cave," painstakingly learned during her fourth and last year of lessons, that she'd never forgotten. It was what the family called her "mood" piece, played in times of stress, or anger, or happiness.

She played it now, over and over, and she thought: Last night was an awakening in more than one way. There was the feeling I had when I thought Rosalie was Georgia. All these weeks I've been so sure of Andy—was I just pretending? I don't really know him as well as I thought. I never dreamed that he would get as mad as he did. Telling him I was sorry didn't help, either. Somehow, I never expected him to be so difficult. How can I know that he won't be again? What a difference a day, or a night, can make. Yesterday I was one person, today I'm another. Yesterday everything seemed so simple, but today life seems uncertain. This piece sounds the way I feel. There's a kind of sadness in it. I wonder if Mendelssohn had problems when he composed it.

It was midafternoon when Liz Perkins and Genevra Coffman drove by and stopped to see her. Jean took them to her bedroom and closed the door. She didn't want her mother, reading on the porch, to overhear any reference to what had happened last night.

Genevra sat on the purple, blue, and white boudoir chair. Liz and Jean sprawled on the matching chintz coverlet of the Jenny Lind bed.

"This is a sweet room," Liz said. But she wasn't really interested in the furnishings. "We were driving past and we thought we'd—" She could wait no longer. "*What* did you think of the beach party?"

"The party was all right," Jean said with significant overtones. "Or it would have been, if—"

"Exactly!" Liz said. "That's what we thought, too!" Her dark eyes were excited, as was her manner. "Honestly, did you *ever,* in your whole *life,* see such a disgusting exhibition?"

"No, I never did," Jean said. "What did the other kids think about it?"

"Tom was mad," Genevra said. Her voice sounded tired and she looked, Jean thought, a little pale. Probably the heat, or maybe she'd been up too late. "He said Garve had no business bringing a girl like that."

"Andy didn't like it, either. He said he didn't know about Garve. I wonder how the guy happened to be included. He never was, before."

Liz shrugged. "Who knows? Just one of those things. And I suppose he was too stupid, or too *canned,* to know that we wouldn't appreciate—," she giggled—"the *treat* he had for us. But wouldn't you have thought the girl, *herself,* would have realized?"

Liz, Jean thought, is an accenter of words. "I believe she did. I felt sorry for her."

"You're not *serious?*"

"I am. Oh, I know she wasn't our kind, and all that, but I don't think she really wanted to dance. Garve made her do it and I can't stand him. He's ten times worse than Rosie."

"Well, he *could* be, I suppose." Liz didn't sound convinced. "I wonder where he found her."

"Tom says," Genevra interposed, "that he understands she's in the floor show at Bailey's."

"That would explain none of us ever seeing her before," Jean said.

"Tom says," Genevra said again, and Liz giggled. "Who is this Tom you're always quoting, Gee?"

Genevra's pale face took on some color. "Oh, hush. Tom says she's nothing but a cheap stripper."

"Well," Liz said, "thank goodness we don't have to associate with people like that. Listen, what are you kids going to wear tomorrow?"

The question lead to a discussion of clothes and fall fashions, of the relative merits of typing as opposed to music for an elective, of the practice scrimmages that had been going on in Mitchell Field for the past two weeks, of what it would be like to have a new gym teacher, of whether Mary Lawrence really liked Jim Wooster or whether she still secretly liked Art Benninger, of whether Virginia Montrie would make it for valedictorian, of Janet Marshall's new hair style, and Tip McGinty's new dog, and the new booths in Grandy's.

These were familiar topics, familiar friends, familiar settings. Before the girls left Jean found that the thought of the girl named Rosalie had been pushed to the background of her mind. Much more absorbing was the thought of school.

CHAPTER ELEVEN

School life quickly became standardized. Within days the excitement of being a senior had vanished. Teachers, it was felt, were making the most of their last chance to impart knowledge to these particular students. Homework mounted, and every night Jean lugged home a stack of books and notebooks so high that her arms ached from carrying them.

She never quite finished what she outlined for herself as an evening of studies. "Of course," Bill said to her, "if you spent half as much time on your lessons as you do on some of these long-winded telephone conversations you have with your friends—what *do* you girls talk about?"

She didn't tell him that one of the long-winded telephone conversations she had each night was with Andy. This was a part of going steady, to know that he would call her, even though they saw each other daily in school. She'd never had many telephone talks with boys. There had been some, but never any that had been other than a request for a date, or for a school assignment. Nor had she been one to take the initiative and call boys, as lots of girls did. Andy had commented on this. "I'm glad you don't bother a guy all the time," he'd said. "Some girls can really drive a boy crazy." He'd added, grinning, "Don't call me, I'll call you."

And so he had, every night. She discovered that the telephone cord was just long enough to reach from the hall to the top of the basement steps and so, by shutting the door, she could speak to him in privacy, regardless of how near other members of the family might be. It was sheer pleasure to talk thus, for they had so little time together in school, and even though Andy drove her to school every morning, what could a person say in five minutes that was important?

She never saw him after school was over for he left immediately for his job at Loblaw's. Sometimes, when she was dawdling in Grandy's with Virginia and Susy and Liz, she thought of him checking stock, or trimming off the brown outer leaves of lettuce heads, or weighing bananas and marking prices thereon with indelible pencil, and she would feel that she ought to be accomplishing more. At such times she would go home and offer to help with dinner or with the ironing. These times were rare, however, and usually by the time she reached home she was too tired to do anything but stretch out on the bed. Unless, of course, the telephone rang.

Early in September, when Andy had started showing up on school nights, Mrs. Chelton had laid down what she called house rules. "This is a hard year," she'd said, "for both of you, and there will be no dates through the week except for special occasions."

Andy had chuckled. "You don't know, of course, Mrs. Chelton, that special occasions usually occur *only* on weekends?"

Later he'd said to Jean, "She's right, you know. I like your mother. Your father, too. The things they say make sense."

"They like you, too," Jean had said.

"I hope they keep on. You know, I think we ought to prove to them that we have a little sense, too. We ought to lay down a few rules ourselves."

"Such as?"

"Oh, what time to be in, and maybe spending an evening with them once in a while instead of going out all the time."

"They'd like that. As for time, Mother always allows a reasonable amount for stopping somewhere to eat after the Friday night dance. I think if we're home by twelve-thirty she won't worry."

"Okay. Check with her, will you, and see if it's all right?"

It had been all right. So, on Friday nights, Jean went

72

early to Teen-Inn and Andy met her there, after he'd finished work. Sometimes, when they left, they came directly home, and Andy would stop in the house for ten, or twelve, or twenty-five minutes, depending upon how close the time was to deadline.

"One thing about us," Jean said one night. "We certainly obey our own laws, don't we?"

They were sitting on the sofa and Andy had just inspected his watch. "Yep," he said. "A pair of good citizens in the making, that's us." He whistled a few bars of *The Stars and Stripes Forever* and broke off to add, "Seriously, I like having rules to live by, as long as they're reasonable. I think most kids do."

"So do I."

"Even parent-made ones," Andy went on. He sighed. "Of course, that's where a lot of rules go out of bounds."

"I know. So many parents can be so darned unreasonable."

"Like Genevra Coffman's. I was thinking tonight, when I saw Gee and Tom leave, that that's a heck of a way to have to live. He can't even take her all the way home, you know. He drops her off about two blocks away."

"I know. It's too bad. Gee and Tom are both such nice kids and Gee, for one, hates it. She told me one time that she'd give anything to be able to have Tom come to her house."

"What's the matter? Don't the Coffmans trust him with their darling daughter?"

"I don't think it's Tom specifically that they object to. I think they'd act the same about anyone."

"Then they don't trust Gee."

"No, it isn't that, either. They're just—funny."

"I'll say amen to that. Anyway, it's a darned shame. Believe me, when I'm a parent, I'm going to want my kids to bring all their friends home. I may lay down a few rules, you understand, but I want things on the up and up."

"That's the way things ought to be."

"Sure, that's the way they ought to be. It's also the way they often aren't. And speaking of laws," Andy got to his feet. "I'd better start abiding."

Just as school life came within the confines of a pattern,

73

so did these dates with Andy. At times they talked seriously, at others they just teased, and insulted each other, and even scuffled. More and more often they were spending Saturday and Sunday nights at Jean's home, watching television with the Cheltons, making popcorn, at times studying. When Jean had to mount the one hundred varieties of leaves required for Doc Andrews' Biology course, Andy helped her. He spent one whole Sunday afternoon scouring the woods for the left-turning sassafras needed to complete her collection and arrived at her house brandishing a whole bush. She, in turn, helped him in his struggle with chemical equations and assisted, early one evening, in painting on the side of his car the letters RAM-SHACK.

"It doesn't look right," she said. "It ought to have an L and an E at the end."

"Listen, this old boat's no qualifying adjective. She's a real noun."

"If she is, she's extinct."

"That fits. Some of her parts will never again be duplicated."

"I give up."

"You'll have to. We've run out of paint."

Fun, all of it. Fun, to dash out of the house in the morning at the first beep from the Ramshack's horn, to stash her books in the back seat, to hurtle across town, hunt for a parking place, and race to the high school building. Fun, to know that someone would be waiting for her after the football game, someone would be meeting her at Teen-Inn, someone would be asking her to the Harvest Ball and the Christmas dance. Fun, to say to the other girls, "Andy and I went to the auto show Saturday night." "Andy and I think that the Teen-Inn board ought to establish a scholarship." Andy and I went. Andy and I think. Andy and I did. Andy and I said. Andy and I. Two inseparable words. Two inseparable people.

Bill left for his college on the third Sunday of September. The night before his departure Jean spent at home, without Andy. "It's a kind of tradition in our family," she'd told him. "Whenever one of us goes somewhere, the rest of us get very sentimental. I guess we suddenly realize how much we're going to miss the guy who's going, so we all stay home and our family life becomes anything but normal. No one fights!"

No one fights. She'd made the statement with assurance. Yet, on this particular night, she and Bill had their first argument in weeks. It happened when she went to his room to help him with packing.

She sat on the bed and leaned back on her hands, surveying the opened drawers from which Bill was taking clean shirts and socks and pajamas. "I'll never be able to understand it," she said. "If I were going away to school, I'd have been getting ready all summer. But you wait until the night before and it's a matter of minutes."

"That," Bill said, "is the difference between the male and the female of the species. You take this suit, for example." He hung a lightweight charcoal woolen in his go-bag. "The male is a one-suit, one-hat, one-pair-of-shoes creature. But the female—ha! The female would need a little green number and a lavender job and a salmon, and she would have to have a black, and she would die without a pink, and she wouldn't be caught without a purple, and she—"

"I get it," Jean said. "But you needn't think you're so smart. Did it ever occur to you that the one suit you're so proud of needs a whole lot of shirts? Washed and ironed and with buttons sewn on? And who takes care of that if it isn't the female of the species?"

Bill grinned. "Score." He tossed her a stack of ties. "Here, female, how about folding these?"

She held the ties in her lap. "Bill, what's college like? Really?"

"Hard. Tough. Relentless. You've got to work, or else. Not work the way you understand it, Jean. You high school kids have got it made if you only knew it."

"Oh, sure. We don't do anything but play. We never put together a terrarium, or plan a source paper, or read the *American Observer* and have a panel discussion of current events. Not us. We're the spoiled younger generation."

"Yep," Bill said. "You are. Hey, what are you doing to my ties?"

"I'm knotting them. And it's no more than you deserve."

Bill rescued the ties. "I ought to bop you. But I guess I

won't. You know, Jean, this last night at home always gets me. I even feel mellow about you. I'll probably regret this later, but right now I'm playing with the notion of asking you up for a weekend this fall."

"Oh, Bill, I'd love it."

"Would you?"

"Yes and yes and yes!"

"Well—" Bill untied the last of the knots and laid the ties carefully on top of his shirts. "There's a guy at school who's been wanting to meet you."

"There is?" She felt an unaccustomed quickening of interest. "What's his name? What does he look like? How old is he? Why does he want to meet me?"

"This may not surprise you, conceited as you are," Bill said, "but it certainly threw me for a loss. The guy thinks you're pretty. He's been ogling your picture for the last year, but I told him he'd have to wait until you grew up."

"Oh, Bill you didn't?"

"Sure, I did." His grin was maddening. "Anyhow, he's quite a guy. His name is Allen Lockwood and he wants you to come for a dance. So, if you're a good girl and help Mom sew on those buttons when my shirts come home every week, I might consider fixing it up."

She was lost in a whirl of glowing mental pictures. Somewhere there was a boy named Allen Lockwood who thought she was pretty. A college boy! She was going to a dance with him and she was waiting in the living room of Bill's fraternity house. This perfectly marvelous looking stranger walked into the room. He came directly to her. "I'd know you anywhere, Jean, although I must say—" He leaned back and surveyed her intently. "Your picture doesn't begin to do you justice."

"Well, how about it?"

Bill's voice brought her back to reality. "How about—oh, you mean will I sew on the buttons?"

"Come back, little Sheba. I mean would you like me to arrange it?"

"Bill, I'd love—" She hesitated. Something had been bothering her and she knew suddenly what it was. How could she have forgotten, even for a minute, that she was going steady? Girls who were going steady didn't skip off to college dances with other boys They didn't even *consider* such a thing. Why, then, had she experienced actual pleasure in the thought? Was something wrong with her?

"You're a darling to suggest it. But I can't, of course."

"Why not?"

"I happen to be going steady."

"Bull!" He stared at her. "Jean, you're not still taking this Andy Decker thing seriously, are you?"

"And if I am?"

"If you are, you're riding for a fall."

"I'm doing no such thing."

"Want to bet?"

"Why should I want to bet when there's no need?"

"Because—oh, skip it." Bill slammed the lid on his bag. "No! You listen to me, Jean Alexandra Chelton! You know darned well that for a minute, there, you were as pleased as a Miss America winner, just thinking about coming up for a dance with a guy you don't even know. And that's all right, that's the way it ought to be. What isn't all right is that you're submerging your natural gregariousness and clinging to your underbaked adolescent belief in—"

"Oh!" Jean shouted. She was furious. "And what college professor are you quoting now, Mr. Big Shot?"

"I'm not quoting. I'm telling you. And if you don't have the sense to listen—"

"I'm listening. It's what I'm hearing that doesn't make sense."

"Then," Bill said, "there's not much point in continuing, is there?"

"No, there most certainly isn't. Anyway, if you keep on, you'll be talking to yourself. I'm leaving. You can do your own packing."

"That's what I've *been* doing, for gosh sakes!"

It was too bad, Jean thought later, that Bill had felt compelled to spoil his last evening at home. Usually, when they quarreled, they made up within an hour or two or, at the latest, the next day. But this time there had been no reconciliation. When Bill left, his relations with her were still somewhat strained, although a surface truce, for the sake of the family, had been silently declared.

77

The after effect was troubling, for, in remembering, Jean knew that some of what he'd said had, indeed, made sense. She *had* been as pleased as a Miss America winner. Did this pleasure, then, make her unloyal to the boy she liked? *Ought* she to meet others before settling so permanently on just one? Was she, really, ready?

CHAPTER TWELVE

"Jean," Mrs. Chelton said. "What are you planning on doing tonight?"

It was the last Saturday morning in September, and it was a warm, lazy, Indian summer kind of day, the kind that filled a person with vague longing for the unknown.

"Oh, I don't know," Jean said. She sat at the kitchen counter and watched her mother roll out pastry. "I know what I'd like to be doing. I'd like to be climbing a mountain in Switzerland, or visiting San Francisco's Chinatown, or sitting at a sidewalk café in Paris, sipping one of those—what are they called?—*apéritifs*? Or maybe just riding through Central Park—that's in New York, you know—in a horse-drawn cab."

"You read too much," Mrs. Chelton said. "Personally, what I'd like would be a safari through the Congo." She smiled. "That's in Africa, you know."

Jean was unaware of the teasing. "I know."

"But I'm afraid I'll have to let down a hem in another of Betty's dresses. That child has grown a foot since last year. Well, maybe not a foot, but it seems as though I spend half my life—" She sighed, and lifted the pastry onto a glass plate.

Jean grinned. "Well, at least *I* have stopped growing. Almost, anyway. Tell you what. Maybe I can put the hem in Betty's dress before Andy comes."

Mrs. Chelton fluted the edge carefully and made no acknowledgement of the offer. Maybe she hadn't heard, for her next question had no relation to dressmaking. "By the way, Jean, how's Virginia these days?"

"Virginia? Fine, I guess. I don't see much of her, you know."

"I do know." Mrs. Chelton set the pie plate carefully to one side and dusted the flour from her hands with apparent concentration. "As a matter of fact, Jean, I've been wanting to talk to you about that."

Jean glanced quickly at her mother. She'd detected a tone of voice with which she was familiar. She almost said, "What have I done *now*?" But she kept the question to a thought and said, with seeming innocence, "What do you mean?"

"I mean that we never see Virginia any more. She used to be in and out almost as much as you, but I don't think she's been here once since school started. What has happened, Jean? Have you quarreled?"

"Quarreled? Virginia and I? Heavens, no!"

"Then, why doesn't she come?"

"Oh, Mom, you ought to know the answer to that. It's because I'm going steady and she's not."

Mrs. Chelton rolled out a second piece of pastry. "If that's the answer, it's not a very good one, Jean. It's no excuse for dropping old friends."

"I haven't dropped her. She understands, honestly she does."

"Even so, I can't help but think you're making a mistake. A big one." Mrs. Chelton laid down the rolling pin and looked directly at her daughter. "Jean, the last thing I want to do is make you resentful. I know that what I'm about to say may do just that, and yet I feel that I ought to let you know what I'm thinking."

"I wish you would. Because I *don't* know what it is."

"Very well. You're spending entirely too much time with Andy."

"But, Mom!" Jean's protest was automatic.

"Now, wait a minute, Jean, hear me out. I'm quite concerned about the fact that Virginia never comes here any more. I miss her, and I should think you would, too. But it isn't only Virginia; none of your friends appear. The only person who comes is Andy, and it just isn't right for you to see no one but him. Friends are important. You need them if you are to become a well-rounded person."

"I've got friends."

"At present, yes. But how long do you expect to keep them if you make no effort? Friendships need care and interest. They don't flourish all by themselves, darling."

Her mother had been right about the resentment, Jean thought. She said, "All right, I'll call Virginia now, if that will make you happy."

"Jean, your attitude makes me anything but happy."

"What do you want, then?"

"I want you to try to understand. To see, for yourself, how much you are missing by shutting off old friends and devoting yourself exclusively to one boy."

"You don't like Andy."

Mrs. Chelton sighed. "I do like Andy. Do you think, for one moment, that I'd treat him the way I do if I didn't? Do you think I'd allow him to fix hamburgers for all of us, or play five hundred with him, or lend him car tools if I didn't like him? No, Jean. I like him and I trust him. I think the way the two of you come in after a dance and sit down and talk with your father and me is rather special. And we love having you here with us on Saturday nights and Sunday nights. But that's another thing that worries me. It's wonderful for us, of course, but for you? You can't really enjoy sitting down with the old folks so much, can you? Wouldn't you like to be with younger people? Don't young people today ever double date?"

"Some of them."

"Why don't you and Andy?"

"Well, most kids don't do it unless they're pretty good friends."

"You see? That's just what I've been telling you."

"No, you don't understand. Girls double date some if the boys they're going with are good friends. Like Gee and Liz, for example. Tom and Leroy both play football and they live close to each other and they've always traveled together. And Mary and Janet double date a lot because of Jim and Tip. But when Mary was going with Art Benninger, she and Janet never even saw each other."

"Well, how about Andy? Who is his particular pal?"

"That's just it. He has no one person."

"I wonder why."

"Too busy. He works all the time, Mother. At

Loblaw's, and at home, and cutting grass, and on his car. He's not like sone of these kids who just fool around all the time." She said it defensively. She felt a sudden need to make Andy, in comparison to others, look superior.

"But surely," Mrs. Chelton said reflectively, "there ought to be someone with whom you children could go out. Or even stay in. We'd be glad to turn over the downstairs to you, Jean, if it's a case of the old folks being in the way. Look, darling, we were young once and we know how it is."

Jean still felt defensive. "You just want to get rid of us. You don't appreciate—why, it was Andy himself who suggested that we ought to spend some time with you, and if you think any other boy I know would make a suggestion like that—"

"Get rid of you, indeed!" Mrs. Chelton banged the rolling pin. "Jean Chelton, don't you ever let me hear you say anything like that again. You know better. If you don't apologize this instant I'm going to send you to your room where you will stay until you come to your senses. I mean it!"

The unexpected vehemence was shocking. Jean stared at her mother, then lowered her eyes. "I'm sorry."

Mrs. Chelton said nothing and, becoming conscious that a mumbled *sorry* was not enough, Jean looked up again to find that her mother was watching her. For an instant Jean felt that she was looking at a stranger whom she hated. Then, with an abrupt crumbling of inner defenses, she began to cry and the hate was gone. It was no stranger who came around the counter and laid a hand on her hair. It was her mother.

The incident was something to think about later. And Jean did. She thought of nothing else for the rest of the day, and she was nettled by the questons that seemed unanswerable. Did all kids occasionally hate their parents? Did parents, at times, hate their children? Were children problems? She had heard parents make laughing comments to other parents about their ability to survive various phases their children were going through. She had always thought the remarks disloyal and unfunny, for she hadn't really believed that parents had any problems other than those dealing with house payments or whether or not

81

this would be a good year to buy a car. Oh, there were minor problems with children, of course, like report cards, and tonsillectomies, and broken sleds, and broken arms, and sudden trips to the emergency room of the hospital. But major matters?

Was she herself a problem to her parents? She had never thought so. She had always considered herself self-sufficient and capable of handling her own affairs. She was sure her family had had, until recently, the same attitude about her abilities. Suddenly, they seemed to have ganged up on her. All of them. Bill and her mother both acted as though they didn't trust her to think for herself. And it wasn't fair! All she'd done to warrant this sudden meddling was to start going steady. But three fourths of the kids in high school did that! And other parents—well, most of them, anyway—didn't object. Only hers. How about Andy's mother? How did she feel?

She asked Andy, that night, when they went out in Ramshack. When Andy had arrived, she'd headed him off before he'd had a chance to hang his jacket in the hall. "I think we'd better go out for a while."

He'd looked questioning, but he'd said only, "We can't go far. Not on two gallons of gas."

"We won't have to. But I want to talk, Andy."

He drove to the west end of town and parked the car just off the highway, near a public spring. He turned to face her. "All right, Angel, let's have it."

"Andy, I've had the worst day. I've fought with Mother and I've cried and I've been asking myself questions and I can't seem to find any answers, and I'm—"

"Listen," Andy said. "You're not using me to get even with your mother, are you? I mean, if you had a fight, you didn't just duck out tonight without letting her know, did you? Because I won't get involved in something like that. I'll take you right straight home again."

"No, it isn't that. We made up. At least, I think we did. And she knows I'm with you. But—" She couldn't seem to find the right words.

"But what?"

"Andy, do you ever think we ought to go out more with—well, with other kids?"

"What's the matter? Getting bored with me?"

82

"No. But Mother thinks—well, she thinks we should."

"Why?" He seemed surprised.

"I'm not sure, but she has this crazy idea that it isn't normal, or something, for us to spend all our spare time together, and never have any of the kids over. She can't understand why we like to stay home so much with just her and Dad and Betty."

He grinned a little. "Well, finances have something to do with it, of course. But I thought she liked me. I like *her*. And your Dad, too."

"She does like you."

"Then I guess I don't get it. Unless—well, it could be that we're something of a nuisance, hanging around all the time."

"She says we aren't. It's hard to explain. Her objection doesn't come from their angle, but from ours."

Andy looked thoughtful. "And we don't object. Well, maybe she has a point. I never gave it any thought, I just went ahead and made myself at home and thoroughly enjoyed the making. You see, Jean, I've never had much home life. No brothers or sisters, and no father since I was a kid, and Mom working all the time—"

"Your mother," Jean said. "How does she feel about your going steady?"

"Hard to say. We don't talk much, Mom and I."

"But she knows, doesn't she? I mean, about me?"

"Oh, yes, she knows. But—" Andy stopped and put the fingertips of both hands together. "Let me see if I can explain. Mom and I have had to hustle ever since I was a kid. Believe me, Jean, when you've got to *make* a living in order to *keep* living, there's very little time left over for anything else. At first, when my father died, Mom took over most of the responsibility. But gradually, through the years, more and more of it has been shifted on to me. I'm not complaining, you understand, because that's the way the breaks have gone for us, and maybe some day they'll start going the other way. But responsibility makes a kid grow up darned fast. I told you, once, that I've thought of myself as the man of the family for years. I'm no *boy*, Jean. Not in the sense that Tom and Leroy and some of those kids who've had everything handed to them are. I've earned the right to make my own decisions, and Mom never questions them. Maybe, at times, she's too tired to question them, but whatever I do in my leisure time is okay with her. The friends I choose are okay. And the girls I go with." He smiled at her. "There! Does that answer your question?"

"Yes, Andy, it does."

"Then maybe this will answer another. Going with you has given me a glimpse of something I've never had. For me it's been really great to talk baseball with your father, and ride Betty around on my shoulders, and ask your mother for a piece of her cherry pie. All the things you just take for granted. Actually, I've been feeling like a member of your family. But I'm not. And so—" He flexed his hands. "We'll go out with other kids, Jean, if that's what your parents want. They've given me so much I'd be a dog *not* to respect their wishes."

Jean could only look at him. No one would ever see this boy as she was seeing him. No one would ever hear, in exactly this way, the things he had just told her. No one would ever understand that love could happen so quickly.

But it had. On a Saturday night in late September, while sitting in a car parked just off the road, near a public spring, Jean Chelton looked at the boy beside her and knew. This was no longer a crush. She loved Andy Decker.

OCTOBER

CHAPTER THIRTEEN

October days were full-colored. People drove for miles to view the vivid foliage in the mountain forests. In town, the Farmer's Market, set up on a street intersection near Loblaw's, featured the last of the corn, and glass jars of clear red jelly, made earlier in the season, and wooden boxes of combed honey, and glistening purple eggplant, and green acorn squash, and bunches of golden marigold, and long-stemmed yellow chrysanthemums.

Housewives were removing screens from windows and

taking from various storage places the woolens to which a moth-ball aroma clung. The light-weight summer curtains were coming down and were being replaced by patterned draperies of heavier texture. The porch and patio furniture still visible looked worn and dusty and forgotten.

Daylight saving time would be in effect until the end of the month but people no longer cared, nor argued about whether it was a good thing. Gone was the indolence of summer. If a body wanted to argue he could find more stimulating topics.

School activities were fully scheduled and organized. The football team was having a mediocre season and there was the usual grumbling as to nonsupport, the usual speculation as to the abilities of the coach, the usual condemnation of the player who was known, on the word of seventeen firsthand witnesses, to have broken training. The Drama Club was already rehearsing for the first play, the Chemistry Club and the F.T.A. had settled their conflict over which had prior reservation for the gym on a specific night in November. The yearbook staff had gone to work and was having a problem in rescheduling forgotten appointments for class portraits. The majorettes practiced routines in the music room. The cheer leaders practiced routines in the gym. The choir practiced songs in the auditorium.

Students listened, with a this-has-nothing-to-do-with-me attitude, to guidance period talks on study habits. They listened, with care, to Doc Andrews' explanation of human physiology. They listened, with resignation, to Miss Henderson's insistence that it paid to increase word power. They listened, with interest, to class panel discussions of current events, and, with boredom, to a paid lecturer who talked of Indonesia. They gossiped, they chewed gum, they argued, they complained, they wrote notes, and, unbelievably, they learned.

For Jean Chelton these October days were the ones in which her love for Andy Decker became as golden as wheat. Everyday experiences became intensified. Her senses seemed to have an awareness that was totally new. The smell of bacon frying in the mornings was something to be enjoyed to the fullest. The sight of a blue haze hovering over the mountain tops in the distance stirred her with appreciation of beauty. Laughter was a joyous sound. Nothing felt quite so marvelous as the cold stinging wetness of a morning shower. Nothing had ever tasted as good as last night's barbecued chicken. Church was a sacred place intended for worship. School was for learning and attendance was a privilege. Families were wonderful, friends were wonderful, teachers were wonderful, living was wonderful, love was wonderful.

Love. She said to Virginia, one Saturday afternoon, "I didn't know it would be like this."

Recently she had made a special effort to spend some time with Virginia, and today they were at Virginia's house, working on cancer notebooks for health class.

"I didn't either," Virginia said. "The awful thing is that ever since we've been studying it, I keep discovering symptoms in myself!"

"You discover—oh, you mean cancer!"

"Why, yes. Didn't you?"

"No. I meant—listen, you don't really have any symptoms, do you?"

Virginia grinned. "Not really, I guess. The lump on my finger turned out to be only a bruise. But for one whole day I was positive."

Jean chuckled. "I know. I saw Mrs. Johnson the other day and she'd lost so much weight I was sure about her until I learned she was on a diet."

Virginia traced a red felt C and began to cut it. "What were you talking about when you said— what *was* it you said?"

"I said I didn't know it would be like this. And I didn't mean cancer, I meant love."

"Oh," Virginia said. "Andy." She pasted the felt letter on the white cloth cover of her notebook, then added, "What is it like, Jean?"

Jean propped her elbows on the table and considered. "It's hard to put in words. It's a kind of inner knowing. And it's not because a boy has a cute smile, or is a marvelous dancer, or plays halfback, or any of those things. It's because he *is*, period. Does that make sense?"

"It sounds all right," Virginia said. "I don't have much experience in these things." She added, making it a ques-

86

tion, "I suppose it follows, then, that Andy feels the same way about you?"

Jean opened her notebook and closed it again. She said thoughtfully, "I'm not sure. At times I am, but he's never actually said anything." She smiled. "Our conversations are apt to be limited to what's wrong with the Ramshack's manifold system. But for the present, at least, it's enough for me just to be with him."

It was on the following night that Jean and Andy went to Liz Perkins' home. Liz called in the afternoon and said, "I have a date with Leroy tonight. Why don't you and Andy come over?"

"Why, thanks, Liz," Jean said. "We'd love to."

She was a little surprised. Liz wasn't a particularly close friend. Not in the way Virginia was. And they'd never double dated. Still, it would be something to do. It would also prove to her mother that she and Andy were trying.

As an excursion in double dating, the evening was disappointing. Liz took them to the rumpus room in the basement and Jean's first thought was that Liz was a lucky girl. The pine paneling and bright plaid curtains were gay and informal, the comfortable chairs and the stereo were plus assets. To have all this, and a tiny kitchenette and a powder room and a small extra room for a Ping-pong table, too, was to have a perfect setting for fun.

But Leroy and Liz had apparently been quarreling just before their arrival, for Leroy sat across the room from Liz, a sulky expression on his face, and, after greetings were exchanged, said nothing. Liz tried to cover up by chattering brightly, but when Leroy said, "Oh, for gosh sakes, Liz, give your mouth a rest," she whirled on him in anger. "Well, somebody has to say *something*. What do you expect us to do? Play Quaker Church?"

Jean and Andy looked at each other in embarrassment, and Jean, in a pretense of not having noticed, said, "Where's Gee? I thought she and Tom might be here."

"I called her," Liz said, "but she isn't feeling well."

Which explains, Jean thought, why she asked us. It didn't help the situation to know that they were second choice. Perhaps the quarrel stemmed from that very thing. Leroy probably hadn't wanted them, although it was he who said, a few minutes later, "Come on, Decker, I'll beat you at a game of Ping-pong."

"That ought to be easy," Andy said.

Jean thought: Leroy is insufferable! I hope Andy blitzes him! She and Liz followed the boys into the other room and watched. It soon became obvious that Andy was no match for his opponent. Leroy took the set easily and some measure of good humor was restored, for he laid down his racket and said to Jean, "How about you girls?"

"Yes," Jean said. "I'd like a game. Liz?"

"Okay."

I'll beat her, Jean decided. I must!

But she didn't.

They listened to records then, and Liz, obviously still smarting from Leroy's earlier rebuke, pointedly ignored all of his requests and consulted Andy for selections. Later Leroy said, "Don't you think we ought to have something to drink?"

"You know where the drinks are," she said, and turned her back on him.

Leroy made no move. *"You're* the hostess."

Liz glared at him, then turned to Andy and Jean. "Would you care for something?"

"No, thanks," they said simultaneously, and Jean wondered if Andy was as parched as she. Then she wondered why Liz had asked the question, for the answer made no difference. Liz strolled to the refrigerator, removed three bottles, and served Jean and Andy. With a significant glance toward Leroy, she uncapped the third and drank from it.

Leroy said, "Of all the exhibitions of rudeness I've ever seen—"

"I'm only," Liz said, "following your very excellent example."

They were off, then, as though a sparring bell had been sounded, each deliberately trying, and succeeding, to hurt the other by the things that were said.

Jean and Andy became completely silent, not because they wanted to listen, but because they didn't know what to do. They waited, staring uncomfortably at the floor, until Liz finally said, or rather, shouted, "Leroy, shut *up!* What are Jean and Andy going to *think?*" She turned to them. "I'm sorry. It's just that I get so darned *mad* at this bloke."

"Yeah," Leroy said. "Don't pay any attention to us." Now that the energy of anger had been expended he seemed more truculent. "We'll get over it."

"Oh, that's all right," Jean said.

"Sure," Andy said. "Think nothing of it. Happens in the best of circles."

"Well—" Leroy said. "How about—" His grin was embarrassed. "Would you like something to drink?"

"No, thanks," Andy said. "Look, I hope you won't think we're ducking out, but tomorrow's a school day, and—"

"Sure," Leroy said. "Well—"

"Well—" Jean said, and she thought: Why do we all stand around saying *well*? What's it supposed to prove? "Thanks for everything."

Goodnights were awkward and, in the car, Jean said, "Wasn't that awful? I thought we'd never get away."

"Quite a battle," Andy said. "Let's ride around a while, shall we? And breathe in the old ozone? Brother! I need it!"

"So do I. What hit them, do you think?"

"Nothing out of the ordinary. They fight all the time."

"They do?"

"Sure. But they make up again. Right now they're probably necking like crazy and telling each other it won't happen again. But it will. It's the story of their life!"

"Not much of a life. I wouldn't think, if they fight so much, they'd stay together."

"I know. It doesn't make sense." Andy made a sudden turn with the car, and added, "It's probably just habit."

This was a new thought. "But," Jean said, "if it's just habit, they ought to break it."

"That's harder to do than you might think," Andy said. "They've been going together for a long time."

Jean thought suddenly of Georgia. It had taken Andy, by his own admission, several months to break with Georgia, and they, too, had fought a lot. Did all couples who went steady do so only because they were used to each other? No, not all.

"Jean," Andy said. "Do you mind if we go parking? I
89

want to talk, but I want to be able to look at you while I'm doing it."

"I don't mind." It would be all right. Andy wanted to talk. And even if he kissed her, that would still be all right. But she hoped that he wouldn't choose Breck Hill.

He didn't, although obviously the secondary road cutting off from the main highway was not new to him. Nor did he need help, a mile farther on, in locating the short lane that stretched to the river. The place looked, Jean thought, like the kind of spot in which fishermen sometimes parked their cars before scrambling down over the banks to try their luck with bass. But she doubted if Andy was familiar with it as a fisherman.

The river, from where they sat, was just beyond sight. But they hadn't come here to view the river. They faced each other slightly and smiled.

Andy was the first to speak. "Jean, I was thinking tonight, while I was listening to those two coyotes howl at each other, how lucky I am to have a girl like you. I don't think you know how very nice you are."

"You mean because I don't fight? But I did, once."

"So you did. But that was my fault. And, I don't know, I kept thinking what a rough life Liz and Leroy have ahead of them, and I got to thinking how much different it would be with us, and I—Jean, what about us? We are for *sure,* aren't we?"

She didn't have to ask him what he meant. She loved him. "Yes, Andy, we are for sure."

He seemed driven by a necessity to explain. "I mean, when I think of the things that *could* happen I go crazy. You'll be going to college next year and I'll be in the navy, if the navy'll have me, and we're going to be separated whether we like it or not. After this year is over it's going to be a long old time before we can get together again, do you know that?"

"I suppose it will. But that won't matter, Andy, as long as we know. We can write."

He clasped her hand. "Letters. What happens if I'm off in Thailand and get one of those *Dear John* kind?"

"You won't."

"I might. You're going to be meeting some very sharp boys, Jean."

"Well, don't sailors have a reputation for girls?"

"Not this sailor. This sailor has *got* a girl."

"And this girl has got a sailor."

"I'm serious, Jean."

"Do you think I'm not?"

"I hope you are. Believe me, I was never more serious in my life. I never thought about anyone the way I think about you. I know I'm not half good enough, but as far as I'm concerned, this is the real thing."

"It is for me, too, Andy."

He said, then, what she'd been waiting, since the end of September, to hear. "You understand that I'm not speaking about what Liz and Leroy have; what most kids our ages have? You do know that I love you?"

"I know."

"How?"

"Because I love you."

His kiss was all that it should be. Never again would there be one quite like it.

CHAPTER FOURTEEN

On Monday morning Jean's alarm clock did not go off. She had set it for six o'clock, intending to get up and study for a scheduled test in Problems of Democracy, but she had forgot to pull the button. Last night she'd been in no mood to study. She had seen no point in trying to read the *American Observer* when all she could think about was Andy. Anyway, she would do better on the test if she studied in the morning. The material would be fresher in her mind. Or so she reasoned.

It was Betty who awakened her by charging into her room. "Jean, have you got—aren't you *up* yet? You'd better hurry! You're going to be late. Have you got a quarter? I need a quarter. Today's stamp day, and if I don't get one today I can't fill my book."

"What time is it?"

"Ten minutes to eight. Listen, have you got a quarter?"

"Ten minutes to eight?" Jean jumped out of bed; began searching for clothes. "Why didn't someone call me?"

"Someone did. Mom's been yelling at you for the last half hour. Jean, look in your wallet, will you?"

"For heaven's sake!" Jean shouted. "How do you expect me to find a quarter when I can't even find my shoes?"

"You don't have to act so darned mean," Betty said, but she retreated. "All I did was ask for a quarter!"

Why do these things happen to me? Jean wondered. This, of course, was the morning when the toothpaste tube was empty. This was the morning when, after finally getting dressed, she discovered that the hem had pulled out of her skirt. This was the morning that her favorite red lipstick was missing and she had to wear a shade that clashed with her sweater. This was the morning when she tripped on the stairs and bruised her forearm. This was the morning when she couldn't find her books. This was the morning when Andy wasn't coming for her. He'd had to go early to school, and she would have to run.

The test was scheduled for the first period. She looked at the purple-inked ditto copy passed to her by the instructor. Ten true and false questions, with a rating of five points each. How unfair could Mr. Malon get? Fifty one-point questions would give her a chance, but this! She knew none of the answers and it was with a dreadful feeling of inadequacy that she marked, in order, two plus signs, three zeros, then alternate pluses and zeros to the end.

Three days later, when Mr. Malon returned the papers, she learned that her failure was a certainty. She had made three correct guesses, which gave her a score of fifteen. She hid the paper quickly in her textbook. She could tell by the pleased expression on other faces that results were, for the most part, gratifying. Mr. Malon was talking. "There were five failing grades, one of which surprised me greatly."

Was he looking at her? She was sure he was. She hoped that Virginia hadn't noticed. "I shall be happy to give a retest tomorrow night after school to any students who wish to try for a passing grade."

She was grateful. She'd laughed, with others, about the way this teacher gave retests. "He likes giving them," kids said. "He doesn't have anything else to do."

Now, for the first time, Jean thought: He doesn't have to do it. It can't be any fun, and it certainly means more work for him. He must be what people call a dedicated teacher.

She was sure of it the next night when, after turning in her paper, she thanked him. His eyes, behind heavy-lensed spectacles, blinked at her. "You know, of course, Miss Chelton, that your first paper was a disappointment to me."

This was another thing kids laughed about—the way he addressed them as Mr. and Miss. Bill had said that this was customary in college but Jean knew that here in high school Mr. Malon was the only instructor to do it. She thought: He's paying us a compliment, really, and we don't deserve it. "It was a disappointment to me, too."

"Yes, quite." He blinked his eyes again. He looked absurdly like an owl. "I'm grateful to you for trying again. I have never worked with you before but I'm sure you have above-average ability. That's why I'm so glad you came in tonight. I feel most keenly the tragedy of ability suffering from lack of interest."

"Oh, I'm interested, Mr. Malon. I really like Problems of Democracy."

"Then what happened?"

"I didn't have time to study."

She thought his eyes twinkled, but due to the glasses she wasn't certain. She added quickly, "No, that isn't true. I had the time, but I—just didn't."

"That's what I thought. So, now that we know what the trouble was, we'll have no repetition?"

"Not if I can help it."

She meant it. She would study more. She was a person of above-average ability. Mr. Malon had said so. She would justify his belief in her. She would read every page of her assignments and keep a separate notebook in which she'd jot down the salient points of each paragraph. Then, the next time she had to review for a test, her notebook would give her all the information she needed. It was a wonderful idea. She could hardly wait to begin!

The plan was good but its execution was difficult. For a week she worked diligently, so diligently that for the rest of her life, whenever court procedure was discussed, Jean would be able to quote authoritatively the facts she had learned during this period. Then, one night, she decided that, before she sat down to work, she would have to shampoo her hair. She had just finished when Andy called and, after talking with him for forty minutes, she went to the kitchen for something to eat. There didn't seem to be much in the way of snacks in the refrigerator, but there was a package of gingerbread mix in the cupboard.

She hesitated, then ripped off the box top and poured the contents in a mixing bowl. She would be able to work better after she was fed. While the gingerbread was in the oven she leafed through the new teen-age magazine delivered in that day's mail and found an article on personality building. The *You and Your Problems* section was diverting and she read that while she ate hot gingerbread and sipped cold milk. Finished, she meandered to her bedroom, sat down at her desk, and opened the notebook. But the task ahead seemed too formidable, too time-consuming. She could learn what she had to by skimming through the text without all that laborious copying. Then tomorrow night she would get to work early in the evening and make two days' notes. But the next night the J.V.'s had a football game and Susy wanted her to go and somehow, after that, the notebook was forgotten.

Then, of course, there was Andy. The thought of him was a warm, wonderful accompaniment to everything she did. Being with him in actuality was always new. Now that she knew he loved her, everything about him took on significance. The scar just below his eyebrow was a very special part of him, although he'd laughed when she'd asked him about it. "I'd like to tell you I got it in the Rue Morgue," he'd said. "But the truth is that I fell off my bicycle when I was a kid and got this cut above my eye. I was darned proud of the stitches, though."

She loved the way his green-brown eyes laughed at her, and the way they could shine with seriousness. She loved the lanky look of him; the bouncy way he walked; the monotone in which he sang; the mended, but always clean, shirts. She loved the way he kissed her.

He kissed her a lot after that night when they'd parked near the river. They'd gone there again, several times, and she always felt a little guilty when she told her mother that they'd been out riding around. It was the truth but not the whole truth. What else could kids do on a Saturday night? Dances got boring after a while, and movies cost money, and what was left?

They didn't neck all the time, either. They talked a lot. Andy said, one night, "We never run out, do we?"

"Of what?"

"Things to talk about."

"Why should we?"

"I was just thinking. Lots of girls don't want to talk."

"Maybe they don't know how."

"Could be." He sounded doubtful.

"I mean it. I know girls who are shy."

"Name one."

"Uh—well—there's—"

He laughed. "You see?"

She laughed, too, but later, when she remembered the conversation, it didn't seem quite so funny. He'd sounded very assured when he'd said that lots of girls didn't want to talk. By lots of girls had he meant one girl? Had he meant Georgia?

It was strange that never once, during all the time she had been dating Andy, had she run across Georgia. Of course, Georgia had spent a lot of time at the lake before going away to school and that was probably the explanation. Anyway, what did it matter? Georgia was no concern of hers. Not any more, Not even on the night they drove to the top of Breck Hill.

At first Jean was apprehensive. Suppose someone should see her! What would people say? What would Bill say? She knew the answer to that. She could just hear him. He'd written to her about a week after his return to school and had apologized for blowing his top. He'd said: *You didn't deserve it. You're too good a kid. I'm abject, I'm penitent, in other words, I'm sorry. How about making up so that I can forget you and settle down to passing Applied Psych?*

She'd answered in kind. *I did, too, deserve it. I think! Anyway, consider us made up. Settle down and pass your*

95

psychology, applied or misapplied.

She'd felt a lot better, for she hated conflict with Bill. But now! If he could see her this moment he'd sound off like the noon factory whistle!

Breck Hill was, in a way, disappointing. She wasn't sure what she had expected, but it looked so average. It was just a hill, and, at its summit, a circular dirt road enclosed a small grassy space large enough to accomodate three or four cars. The headlights made visible, within the circle, a trash can and a few blackened stones where a fire had once been built. The view, though, was superb. A good portion of the town could be seen from here and, at night, the street lights looked like an exhibit of jewels laid out in unplanned pattern.

Andy dimmed the Ramshack's lights. "Ever been up here before?"

"No."

"You haven't?" Then he answered his own question. "No, I guess you haven't." He turned toward her. "Let's talk. Tell me about you."

"What can I tell you that you don't already know?"

"Millions of things. Tell me what you know about the stars, if anything. Tell me about when you were little. Tell me about your most embarrassing moment, or your happiest one, or your most let-down one."

His mood tonight was the one she liked best. "Well," she said, "the most let-down one I ever had was when I ran away from home."

"Chelton, you are a constant amazement to me. When did you run away from home?"

"When I was eleven years old."

"Why?"

"Because I wanted to go to the movies with Virginia, and Mother wouldn't let me. So I went upstairs and packed my overnight bag and when I came down I announced to the family that I was leaving forever."

"No kidding? What did they do?"

"Nothing. Mother said, 'Oh, is that so? Good-by, then,' and Dad said, 'Have a good trip.' They didn't even come to the door with me, and I went out and walked for eight blocks. The bag got heavier and heavier and by the time I came to the school playground I was licked. There wasn't a soul there, and I sat on a bench for a while. I was cold and I was hungry, and finally I decided that my parents had probably learned their lesson. I pictured Mom as crying, and Dad as pacing the floor, and maybe calling the police to institute a search. I was sure they'd be so glad to see me that in the future they would allow me to go to all the movies I wished to see. I thought they would even give me extra money for banana splits."

Andy chuckled. "And did they?"

"Not at all. When I got home the door was locked. I stood in front of it and I didn't know what to do. My pride was hurt, but the hunger was worse, so I rang the bell. Mother answered, and all she said was, 'Back so soon?' She didn't scold me, but she didn't feed me, either. I got the feeling that no one had cared, no one had even missed me, so I went to bed. Talk about a let-down kid, that was me!"

"Did you ever try it again?"

"After an experience like that? There was no point."

"Your parents are smart. I have a lot of respect for them, Jean."

"I'm glad."

"I mean it. I would never do anything to hurt them. Say, did I ever tell you about the time Tom Evans and I set out with Geiger counters to seek our fortunes?"

"No."

"That was quite a deal. It lasted only as long as our food held out. The counters weren't even real and the uranium was nonexistent. We got mighty excited, though, when we found a piece of quartz."

They talked for an hour. Then Andy said, "It's getting cold. What do you say to heading back to town?"

"I'm with you."

He smiled at her. "As if I didn't know."

Jean's answering smile was partly for him, but partly for herself. She thought, as Andy started the car: This is really funny. No one would believe that I've been parked on Breck Hill for an hour and haven't even been kissed!

CHAPTER FIFTEEN

In late October two separate and wholly shocking incidents occurred.

The first happened on the day the six weeks' report card came out. Jean had received an E in Problems of Democracy. Her first reaction was one of disbelief. Not a red mark! Not for her! Someone had made a mistake. Her home-room teacher had put the grade on a card intended for another student. Either that, or Mr. Malon had reached an incorrect total in adding points. She would check with him right after school, for she certainly couldn't take home a report like this.

Mr. Malon said, "No, Miss Chelton, the total is correct." He blinked. "Here, you can see for yourself." He opened his grade book and showed her.

"But I made up that fifty point test, Mr. Malon, and I thought—"

"You brought your grade only to passing, Miss Chelton. And you failed to make up the next one. So—"

"But I'm only one point under a D!"

"That's right. Just a little extra effort, Miss Chelton, can make a big difference, can't it?"

Her notebook. If she'd kept on with her notebook—well, no sense in crying over that. Still it wasn't fair. Another teacher might have written in the one extra point she'd needed. Miss Polti would have, she was sure. But not Mr. Malon. Oh, no, he had to stick by rules and regulations, darn his blinky old eyes!

All the way home she rehearsed what she would say to her parents. She would have to show them the report, for Betty would bounce in full of pride over a card that would probably show straight A's.

She was right in her forecast. Her mother was admiring Betty's report when Jean walked into the kitchen, and Betty's first words were, "What did you get, Jean?"

"Not what you did, I imagine," Jean said. "Mine's awful!"

Mrs. Chelton smiled. "Oh, I doubt if it's as bad as you make it sound. Let's have a look."

There was nothing to do, of course, but hand it over.

Mrs. Chelton studied the card. Then she said, "I see." She replaced the card in its envelope and tapped it on the edge of the counter. "We'll talk about it later, shall we?"

Reprieve, Jean knew, was only temporary. Until the ultimatum, though, she would exhibit her best behavior. "Is there anything I can do to help you, Mother?"

She performed her usual tasks. She set the table, and made the salad, and peeled the potatoes. She contemplated, but did not follow through on, the chore of cleaning the silver. Still, even to think of such a thing gave her a virtuous glow. She was very polite. When Betty charged through the kitchen and bumped her, causing her to upset a bottle of milk, she did not yell, but said, "That's all right, honey. It was an accident."

When her father came home she was upstairs, straightening the towels on the bathroom racks. She heard him say, "What's that you've got, pudding?" and knew that Betty had met him at the door. "My, my," he said next. "What have we got here, a budding genius?"

She heard the door bang as Betty went outside. She heard her mother speaking in a low voice. This time she couldn't hear what was said, but she knew.

When dinner was over Mr. Chelton said, "Betty, your mother and Jean and I have something we want to talk over. Don't you have some homework you can do in your room?"

"It's all done," Betty announced. "I haven't got a thing to do." Usually she was the first to be excused, but now she settled back in her chair and folded her hands in her lap.

"But this is private talk, dear. You know what private means don't you?"

"Of course. It's like general only it's at the other end of the army."

Mr. Chelton chuckled. "A darned good definition. Except that this isn't the army, this is the family, and private in this case means that we want you to go to your room."

"But I'm part of the family. Why can't I get in on it?"

"Because—" Mr. Chelton floundered and sent a silent appeal to his wife.

"Because this concerns Jean, not you," Mrs. Chelton said. "I'll tell you what. Some day, when we have something to say to just you, we'll make Jean go to her room."

"We-ell," Betty folded her arms. "Promise?"

"On my honor as the mother of a Brownie scout."

"Oke." Betty got to her feet. "I guess you'd better cross your heart and hope to die, too, just to make sure."

"I cross my heart and hope to die," Mrs. Chelton said. "The very next time something comes up."

When she had gone Mr. Chelton took a final sip of coffee. "Your mother told me about your Problems of Democracy grade, Jean. I'm sorry. Before I start issuing orders like a guy at the top end of the army—" he smiled—"I think we ought to hear your side of it. What's your explanation for what happened?"

Jean fidgeted. "All I did was fail a couple of tests. But I made one of them up. And honestly, Dad, no one gets a good grade in P.O.D. Mr. Malon only used a hundred points for the whole six weeks, and he makes seventy-five percent his passing grade, and nobody got higher than a B, this time. Why, Janet Marshall has always had A's in everything, and she got a D. And Jim Wooster and Leroy Arnst only got—"

"I'm not interested in a roll call, Jean. I am interested in helping you. A failing grade is serious. You're a senior. You want to be graduated, don't you?"

"Of course."

"All right, then. We've got a problem. There can be no repetition, you understand that, I'm sure. If you were a poor, or even a mediocre student, it would be different. But you're not. This is the first time you ever had anything lower than a C, so we know that you're capable. And your mother and I—well, we wouldn't be living up to our responsibilities as parents if we didn't help you solve your problem. So, first off, we've got to find out *why* you failed. That's logical, isn't it?"

"Yes, I suppose so. But I don't *know* why."

Mr. Chelton said, "Sit on a log for a few minutes. We'll wait."

The reference to the log was familiar. It had to do with one of his favorite stories and it meant that she was supposed to think. But where could she start? What was wrong? Why had she failed, really?

She hadn't known the answers to test questions. Take it a step farther. Why hadn't she known them? Lack of preparation. Why hadn't she been prepared? Lack of time. Why hadn't she had time? Too busy. Too busy doing what? Thinking. Of Studies? No. Of Andy.

Jean stared at her dessert bowl. Her problem was within herself. Love was no excuse for failure. She'd been whirling within a golden bubble of dreams. But passing grades were not secured by dreams, they were made by work. The time for dreams was after work had been completed, not before. Her father was right. There could be no repetition. She said, "I do know why. Do I have to tell you?"

Mr. Chelton looked at his wife and she said, "If you know why, you also know how to correct the situation. Do you need help?"

"No."

"Then I don't think you need to tell us. I believe you'll do better if you work this out for yourself, without any interference from us. Don't you agree, William?"

Mr. Chelton nodded. "Completely. We have confidence in you, Jean. I'm sure your next six weeks' report will show that the confidence was not misplaced. Now, how about another cup of coffee?"

That night, when she was preparing to study, Jean thought about her parents. She was proud of their confidence. She was going to work hard. She couldn't do otherwise when their attitude was so superb. Lots of parents would have bribed, or threatened, or lectured. But hers had done the best possible thing by making her figure it out for herself. Had their attitude been different she might have been feeling resentful. As it was, though, all she felt was a desire to improve. She opened her P.O.D. book and began to read.

There were only three days left in October when the second thought-provoking incident occurred. This time Jean was not directly involved, but she was stunned by what she heard. Everyone was. The whole student body talked excitedly, and speculated, and gossiped. All conversations started with "Did you know?" or "Have you heard?" or "What do you think?"

The reason for the turmoil was a sensational bit of news. Genevra Coffman was leaving school. She wouldn't return. She was going to have a baby.

It was Liz who relayed the information to Jean at the start of the school day. Jean was stricken. "Oh, no!" she said. "Not Gee. It's one of those awful rumors that go around. It just couldn't be true!"

"It's true," Liz said. "Her things are gone from her desk. She won't be back."

"It could be something else. Her family could be moving, or—or—maybe rheumatic fever, or—"

"No. Jean, hadn't you noticed anything? I mean, she's been absent so much, and several times she's had to be excused from class. I went with her to the lav one day and, honestly, she gagged until I thought she would choke! And she hasn't worn a straight skirt since school started."

"I never noticed a thing," Jean said. But she remembered suddenly that she had. She'd noticed several times how pale Gee had been; how tired she had looked. She had never suspected this, though. "It's incredible." Then she added, "I suppose the boy is Tom?"

"Who else?"

"What's he going to do?"

"I don't know. Neither of them is here, today. Look, it's almost time for the bell. We'll talk later, okay?"

All day Jean was conscious of inner turbulence. It was impossible to dismiss the thought of Gee Coffman. In several of her classes, because of the alphabetical assignment, she was confronted by an empty seat next to her own. Not that she needed a reminder but the vacant seat seemed so desolate. What a tragedy it was! Here had sat a girl whose life ahead could have been superb! She'd been active in school affairs—she'd been a member of student council, and a majorette, and vice president of her class. She'd been smart, too. She'd made National Honor Society last year. But even more important, perhaps, she'd been so nice, and so friendly, always, to everyone. Things like this didn't happen to girls like Gee Coffman. They happened to the dumb ones, the crude ones, the ones like—well, like that Rosalie, for example, whom Garve had brought to the picnic. You expected these things of girls like that! Not of girls like Gee! And Tom Maheney—why, Tom had been terribly disgusted that night of the beach party. What had happened? Why Gee? And why Tom?

"I can't understand it," she said to Liz after school. They were sharing a booth in Grandy's with Virginia, and they'd been discussing what she supposed all the other kids in all the other booths were discussing. "It isn't like Gee. Do you suppose she didn't know what she was doing?"

Liz looked at her. "Oh, Jean, for heaven's sake, grow up. This is the age of enlightenment. Of course, she knew what she was doing. And even if she didn't, Tom must have known."

"Well, I suppose. But they both had so much to lose. Gee won't be graduated, and I know she was planning on college next year. Tom, too. They had nothing to gain by allowing themselves to—" She couldn't finish.

"I'll tell you what *I* think," Liz said. "I think their *parents* are to blame. Tom coming from a broken home the way he does, living with just his mother, and never seeing his father except when he goes to the city to visit him a couple of times a year. And *everyone* knows how strict the *Coffmans* are. I don't think either Tom or Gee have *ever* had any love at home."

"Do you mean," Virginia asked, "that they needed love and so they turned to each other?"

"Exactly!" Liz said. "Don't you agree, Jean?"

"Yes," Jean said. "It sounds like a logical explanation." She said it with a feeling of relief. Her perturbance all day had been caused by an inability to reconcile the fact to the people concerned. Viewed from this angle, though, it was not difficult to transfer the responsibility from Tom's and Gee's actions from themselves to their parents. The kids had been driven to it, really. "In a way, it's a kind of justification, isn't it?" she asked.

Virginia said, "I would hardly call it that, Jean, although they're certainly going to need it. Gee, especially. It's the girl who always gets the rough deal in these situations. Her reputation's gone, and even if the boy marries her—and sometimes he doesn't—everyone knows. I should think there would be a terrific feeling of guilt, either way."

"I should think so, too," Jean said.

"And, of course," Liz added, "there's the actual *having* of the baby. I understand that that is no fun."

"I wish," Jean said, "that we could do something. Do you suppose we might stop by and tell her how sorry we are?"

"Too embarrassing," Liz said. "And, anyway, what do you bet the Coffmans will want to act as though nothing had happened? They'll get her out of town, or something, and—and—I get so darned *mad* when I think of the way they've *treated* her! The whole thing is their fault; no one can convince me that it isn't. Listen, you kids, it's time to shove." She rummaged in her clutch bag. "Can either of you lend me a quarter? I have to buy a notebook cover and I've only got fifty cents. I'll pay you back tomorrow."

She used to borrow from Gee, Jean thought. And Gee from her. Well, that's all over now.

The next day, when the girls met again at Grandy's, Liz had something new to report. "I went to see Gee last night."

"You did?" Jean felt betrayed. "But I thought you said—I mean, I'd like to have gone with you, Liz."

"It's just as well you didn't. She'd been crying a lot, I think, and she didn't have much to say. Honestly, it was just awful. I was always her *closest* friend, and we just didn't seem to have a *thing* in common. I mean, I couldn't talk about *school,* could I, when she's no longer going? And I could hardly *ask* her about—well, *you* know."

"Did she say anything at all about it?" Jean didn't like asking the question but she wanted to know.

"She never said a word until I was ready to leave. And then she said, 'Thanks a lot for coming, Liz.' And all of a sudden she absolutely *crumpled* and she said, 'Oh, Liz, don't ever, ever—' and then she cried. Honestly, I never *saw* so many tears."

"Did she mention Tom?" Virginia asked.

Liz sat up straight to deliver her grenade. "Yes. It seems that Tom wants to marry her but her parents forbid it. They say, *get* this, that she can't rectify one mistake by making another. Isn't that just *like* them?"

"But what do they expect her to do?" Jean asked.

Liz shrugged. "Mrs. Coffman's got a sister who lives in Philadelphia. Gee's supposed to go there next week. And after the baby comes, who knows?"

"Adoption, maybe," Virginia suggested.

"Maybe. Anyway, the whole thing's a *mess. Everyone's* talking about it. You should hear my *parents* on the subject."

"I know," Jean said. "Mine, too. They seem to think the whole thing came about as a result of going steady. But they just don't understand."

NOVEMBER

CHAPTER SIXTEEN

November was cold and gray and bleak. Until the snows came there was a bitterness in the atmosphere that seemed to permeate to the very marrow of a person's bones. The façades of the houses, particularly in the daytime, had a dreary look about them. There was cold within, too. It was found in drafts creeping under closed doors, in high winds that rattled windowpanes, in the chill of water running from the faucets.

People scanned the skies anxiously and said, "Looks like we'll be getting it any day now." No one looked forward to winter and yet, when it came, there was a marked change in attitude. It was as though the November days without snow were a kind of waiting period, filled with uncertainty, but once the season became official a person knew what to do and could go on about his business.

Now was the time for heavy coats and boots and mittens. Now was the time for fires in the grate and hot warming suppers featuring sauerkraut and dumplings, or savory beef stew, or pancakes with maple syrup.

Students in school were settling down to serious study. October weather had distracted them and they'd been prone to gaze from windows. But who wanted to look outside? There was more warmth and more color right in the classrooms, now artificially lighted from morning to night.

Jean Chelton was doing better work. Her attitude was one of resolve. Sometimes, while listening to her English teacher explaining a particularly difficult passage from *Macbeth*, she thought: I wonder why we have to learn all this. The language of Shakespeare is dead. Who, today, ever heard of gerns and gallowglasses? Who cares? She listened, though, and did extra research. The research paid off. She learned, one morning, as the class listened to a recording of the first act, that she was the only person who knew that *graymalkin* meant a gray cat and that a *paddock* was a toad. It was with pride that she relayed the information to the group for, although the incident was slight, she couldn't help noting the awed reaction. One of the students said, as they were leaving, "Where did you ever learn such a thing? I guess that's what it is to be smart."

The remark gave her a glow which was way out of proportion to its cause and she thought: There *is* satisfaction in knowing. The satisfaction, if not the glow, extended to her P.O.D. class. She never went unprepared now, and she answered test questions with a reasonable degree of certainty. Mr. Malon said, once, "Your work is showing improvement, Miss Chelton. It pays to buckle down, eh?"

You can win, Winsocki, she thought, and for the rest of the day the refrain stayed with her. *If* you only buckle down. How much better it was, how much more secure you felt when you buckled down! Skimming could never give you this assurance.

It was surprising to her that this new-found confidence in her school work made her dates with Andy, and even thinking about him, more enjoyable. Now she didn't even mind the rawness of the November days, but thought of them as being exhilarating. This was a wonderful month! This was a month like no other. This was the month that would be climaxed by Harvest Ball!

"By the way," Andy had said on the third day of November, "I heard some of the kids talking about H.B. this morning. We're going, aren't we?"

"Are you asking me or telling me?"

"Both."

"Then what can I say?"

"What kind of an answer is that? Aren't you going to say, 'Oh, thank you sir! I'd love to, sir'?"

"Oh, thank you, sir, I'd love to, sir."

She thought, afterward: This is one of the rewards of going steady. Last year the Harvest Ball was a sweat-out. I thought no one would ever ask me and, when Barney finally did, I was so happy that I didn't even mind being a little taller. I wonder who will be in the court this year. Mary, probably, and Liz, of course, and Gee would have, if—

Gee was now in Philadelphia and Tommy had gone to live with his father. No one had heard from either of them. "In a way," Jean said to Virginia, "that's the worst part of it. Do they think none of us care?"

"No, I imagine they know that we do. But they must also know that they can't go back to the way things used to be. From now on their lives are bound to be different. Gee's, especially. Maybe they feel that a clean break with the past is best."

"Well, whatever lies ahead for them, I hope they find some happiness."

"So do I."

"It's strange, though," Jean said. "Already people are beginning to forget."

"I know. For a time the kids talked of nothing else. Now everyone's getting excited about Harvest Ball."

"I'm getting excited, myself," Jean said. And she was. But in the meantime there were other things to think about. Tonight's date with Andy, for instance.

He'd said this morning, as he'd driven her to school, "I'm going to be late tonight. The boss said there would be a new shipment to check. Will you mind waiting or do you want to skip Teen-Inn altogether?"

"I won't mind waiting."

"All right. Will you be good and keep the wolves away until I get there?"

"I'll be good."

She thought, as she prepared for the dance that night, I

will be, too. I never get a chance to be anything else. The wolf pack isn't interested. But I don't care. I've got Andy and that's enough for me.

She went to the Y alone. Virginia called to ask her if she wanted to go with the girls but Jean, knowing that Andy wouldn't be there so early, declined, saying that she would be along later.

Since there was no point in hurrying, she delayed getting ready, but now that she was on her way she walked quickly. It was a wintry night but there had been, as yet, no snow. Not much longer before it comes, though, Jean decided, and was glad she was wearing her warm car coat.

Later she wished she hadn't. She wished she'd worn her cashmere sweater and that she hadn't tied a scarf around her head. She wished she'd had sense enough to remove her wraps before walking into the gym to see who was there. She might not have looked quite so much like an immigrant just off steerage!

She wished, for a moment, that she hadn't come to the dance at all, even though she saw immediately that Andy was already here. The reason for her wish was the fact that Andy was dancing with another girl, and the girl was Georgia Kane!

She felt instant panic. What was Georgia Kane doing at a Friday night Teen-Inn? What was she doing? Why, dancing with Andy, of course! Just as she had last summer, and last year, and the year before that. Georgia Kane and Andy Decker. Together. Just as they'd always been. Laughing. Talking. Having fun. And Jean Chelton? Where did she belong? Where she was now, on the edge of the floor, watching. She turned. She wasn't sure where she would go. The coat room? The rest room? Home again?

She wasn't going anywhere. Leroy Arnst was standing beside her. "No girl," he said, "ought to watch her boyfriend dancing with his ex-girlfriend. Not when an ex-boyfriend of one of her girlfriends is around. What do you say, Chelton? We may as well console each other."

She stared at him dazedly. "What do you mean?"

"I'm asking you to dance."

"But I—"

His grin was wise. "Why wait for Andy? He didn't wait for you, did he?"

No, he hadn't waited for her. He'd told her he was going to be late. Had he said it knowing that Georgia would be here; that if he came early he could dance with her? "Well," she said doubtfully, "I guess I might as well." She moved toward his arms.

His grin widened knowledgeably. "Your enthusiasm inspires me. But don't you think you'd better take off your coat?"

When she had hung up the coat and hidden the hateful scarf in its sleeve, she said to him, "Where's Liz?"

"I told you. But never mind. If I told you again, you still wouldn't hear."

"I would, too." But already her thoughts were on other things, other people. Specifically, on Andy and Georgia. She began to rationalize. It had been the unexpectedness of seeing them that caused her this sudden fearfulness and uncertainty. Everything was all right. Everything was just as it had been. Nothing had changed. Andy came earlier than he'd planned, he happened to see Georgia, and he spoke to her. Maybe they exchanged a few words, maybe the music started and he did the polite thing. In a moment the record would come to its end. In a moment Andy's dance with Georgia would come to an end. In just a moment, now . . .

The moment came. Georgia was still talking, but Andy was scanning the crowd. When he saw Jean he smiled and she felt a tremendous softening. Then she saw something that disturbed her. Andy never blushed, but now the back of his neck was red. Why?

She forgot her rationalization of the past few minutes. Andy looked guilty. He *was* guilty! Of what, she wasn't sure, but she had never been so angry, nor so humiliated!

He came to her and Leroy disappeared. "Hi. So you got here."

"Yes." She added nothing.

He watched her. "I got here early."

"So I gathered." Her tone showed some asperity.

"Listen, if you're thinking what I think you're thinking, don't."

She gave him no help but remained silent.

The next record was on and couples were starting to

dance. "Come on," he said. "This is no good. Let's get out of here."

"Why?"

"Chelton, don't be like that. We're going to the snack bar."

She allowed herself to be led. It would be better to have this out right now.

The snack bar was dimly lit, as always. They chose a table for two in the corner and Andy got them each a drink. "Root beer," he said, and tried a smile.

The smile had no effect. "Thank you," she said coldly.

He played with the glass, but he didn't drink. His face, in the blue light, looked pale, and his eyes, as he squinted at her, were dark. "You're mad, aren't you?"

"What ever gave you an idea like that?"

"Not what ever. Who ever. You gave me the idea."

"I? But why should I be mad?"

"Because I was dancing with Georgia."

He'd disregarded preliminary sparring and yanked the problem into the open.

"But I don't care in the least. It's immaterial to me whether you dance with Georgia, or Liz, or Susy, or Virginia, or someone I never heard of." A lie, that. But she thought it sounded properly indifferent.

"Is it? Jean, look at me. Do I really matter so little to you?"

She looked at him. She couldn't see him very well in this light, but she didn't have to. She knew him. She knew his straight hair, and the little scar she had touched, and the occasional mischief in his eyes. This was Andy. And he mattered more than a little. Still she temporized. "I don't own you. You are perfectly free to do as you wish."

"No, I'm not. I happen to be in love with you. Not with Georgia, nor Liz, nor Susy, nor Virginia, nor someone I never heard of. With you. So how can I be free?"

"You were acting freely enough."

"All right, I'm sorry. It was thoughtless of me and I didn't realize how it might look to you until I saw the expression on your face. When I saw how embarrassed *you* were I kind of got that way, myself. Now, listen. Georgia came over to speak to me just after I got here. What was I to do? Pretend I'd never known her? Cut her dead?"

"No. But you didn't have to dance with her, did you?"

"So you *did* mind?"

She hadn't intended to admit it but now it was too late. "How could I help it with everyone standing around watching? I felt like thirteen o'clock."

"If it's any solace to you, that's the way I'm feeling now. I mean it, Jean. I danced with Georgia because, at the time, it seemed the polite thing to do. If I had it to do over, though, you can bet I'd run a crooked mile at the sight of her."

"Why?"

"Why?" he echoed. "Do you think I enjoy this? Explanations aren't much fun. Apologies, either."

"So, rather than explain to me, or apologize, you would stay away from her? And not for any other reason?"

"There's another. I don't really like her much."

"Well!" She felt triumphant, vindicated, and generous. "Why didn't you say *that* in the beginning? It's what I wanted to know."

"It is?" He looked unbelieving for an instant. Then he said, "Why, Jean Chelton! You're jealous! I could throttle you. No, I could kiss you." He started to rise.

"Don't you dare."

He sat again. "I can't believe it. I guess I'll never understand girls. Here I was, feeling noble as all get out because I was dancing with Georgia even though I didn't enjoy it, and all the time you were suspecting me of sinister motives. Well, what happened tonight was purely auld lang syne, you know?"

"I guess so." She was silent a minute. "What did you talk about?"

His eyes sparkled. "I told her I loved her madly."

"And what did she say?"

"She said it was hopeless. That's why I came back to you. Chelton, let's go."

"Where? Back to the gym?"

"No. Home."

She'd have liked to dance with him. Not for the sake of dancing but for the sake of appearances. She wanted everyone, and especially Georgia, to see them together.

She wouldn't mention it, though. If Andy wanted to leave, she would leave. It was enough to be with him again.

His mood changed as they drove home. He was unusually quiet and when he stopped the car, for the first time since they'd been dating, he made no move to get out. The street was still. The houses were still. He turned to her. "Jean," he said, "did you ever wish that there was a part of your life that had never been? Or that, having been, you could forget?"

"No," she said. "Oh, there have been parts I haven't liked, but I don't think I'd wish them away, exactly."

"I would. I'd give anything."

"Andy, if you're talking about what happened tonight, we *can* forget that, you know."

"I'm not talking about what happened tonight," he said. "Or maybe I am. Maybe I don't know what I'm talking about period, but I can't help wishing—oh, well, what's done is done."

"You aren't making sense. I don't follow you at all."

"How could you? I'm not sure I follow myself. I just—" He moved closer. "Jean, I wish I could tell you how I feel about you. You're so sweet and so—so *new*. Darn it, that isn't the word I want, but it's all I can think of. You're gentle, too, which is another crazy description, but you *are,* and I've never known another girl who was, and there are times when I want to just grab you and run off with you into the night." Suddenly his arms went around her. "Jean, I—you do love me, don't you?"

"Yes."

He kissed her. Not briefly, but longer than he ever had before. And she thought: This is wonderful. This is what it means really to love someone and to be loved in return.

Unexpectedly he broke away and held her at arm's length. His voice seemed shaken. "If I were a smoking person I'd say this would be the time for a cigarette."

She was trying to recover from the abruptness with which the kiss had ended. "Why?"

"Oh, *you* know." He regarded her gravely and his own face reflected some kind of inner conflict. Then he said, "No, I guess you don't, do you? Come on, Chelton, out you go!"

Almost before she knew it Jean found that she'd been hustled to her own door. She watched, completely baffled, as Andy ran to the car. He didn't look back, but jumped in and drove quickly away.

CHAPTER SEVENTEEN

On Monday Jean learned that Liz and Leroy had broken up. "He is just too possessive," Liz announced. "He takes me for granted. He thinks he can treat me any way he wants to and that I'll always be there. But I've had it."

The two girls were in the locker room, dressing after a last-period gym class, and Liz threw a tennis shoe into the locker as she spoke. She banged the door shut. "I get so *mad!*"

Jean grinned. "So I hear. When did all this happen? Wait, I believe—it was over the weekend, wasn't it?"

Liz stared. "Friday. But how did you know?"

"I saw Leroy Friday night. He said something about it, but I was so busy worrying about Andy that it didn't sink in."

"Where did you see him?"

"At the Y. I had a dance with him."

"That *stinker!* You mean that while I was home crying my heart out he was having himself a gay old time? I could *annihilate* him!"

"I don't think," Jean said, "that he was having a particularly gay time."

"What did he say?"

"I can't remember exactly. Something about consoling me, or maybe it was me consoling him, I'm not sure."

Liz regarded her with obvious curiosity. "Why should *you* need consolation?"

"Georgia Kane was there and Andy was dancing with her."

"Welcome to my league," Liz said. She sounded pleased.

"No," Jean said hurriedly. "You've got it wrong. Andy only danced once with her."

"Didn't you *care?*"

"Yes, I did. But I got over it. Andy told me it didn't mean anything."

"And you believed him," Liz said. "Well, I wouldn't. I would never be so gullible"

Jean was hurt. "I'm not gullible."

"Yes, you are. You *can't* believe everything a boy tells you, Jean, didn't you know that?"

"I should think it would depend on the boy."

"Meaning, I suppose, that you can believe Andy but that I can't believe Leroy. That's where you're wrong. Boys are all alike and they make me *sick!*"

"I don't agree with you. Right now you think that because you've had a fight with Leroy. But you'll change your mind after you've made up."

"No." Liz walked to the mirror and applied lipstick with care. She turned and faced Jean. Her carriage was erect. "I'm through. Jean, you've heard Leroy when we're together. You know how he is. He seems to think that because we're going steady he can say anything he wants to and get away with it. But it's not only what he says, it's what he does that makes me furious. He has stood me up several times, and he has even dated an out-of-town girl, and then lied about it. I've gone right along putting up with him because—well, because in the beginning, at least, I was just *crazy* about him, and later, after we'd been together for so long, I hated the idea of breaking up. I mean, you get *used* to a person, you know?"

Andy had called it habit. He'd been right, for what Liz was saying was proof.

"And then," Liz went on, "I suppose a girl always hesitates to ditch a boy because she can't help wondering if anyone else will ever ask her out. It's easy for a boy, but a girl has to be so darned *subtle* about getting back into circulation."

"That's true," Jean said. She remembered her own times of wondering.

"But there comes a time," Liz said, "when a girl reaches the limit. I don't care if I'm *never* asked anywhere, I still won't go with Leroy. And if anyone *does* ask me,

114

don't think I intend to forget what I've learned. No boy can *ever* tell me anything I'll believe. As for you, I can't *stop* you from believing Andy, but I think you're crazy if you do."

"I'll remember what you've said." Jean spoke gently. Protest would only cause further disagreement, perhaps anger. Liz, she felt, was speaking from recent hurt. Later, when she had calmed down, she would have better perspective. "And I'm sorry about you and Leroy, I truly am."

"Don't be." Liz swung away and flounced toward the door. *"I'm certainly not!"*

Jean followed. But she *is* sorry, she thought. I can understand why. She must feel awfully alone and sort of lost. I would, if I'd just broken with Andy.

On Friday night, when Andy called for her, he informed her that they would have to walk to Teen-Inn. "The Ramshack's being temperamental again. She refuses to start."

"That Ramshack!" Jean said. "She's a regular prima donna. Come over by the fire, Andy. You look cold."

"I am." He held his bare hands toward the blazing fire. "You'd think the eight-block hike over here would have warmed me, wouldn't you? But it didn't."

She felt instant compassion. His jacket was much too thin. And he'd worn no gloves. He was never dressed warmly enough and yet he spent money on her. Not much, but root beer and hamburg and movie money would add up to gloves, or even a sweater.

Mr. Chelton glanced up from the game of checkers he was playing with Betty. "If your car's out of commission, Andy, you're welcome to ours."

"Thank you, sir, but I'd rather not use it."

"Why not? We never have to use persuasion on Bill. Quite the opposite."

"That's different. I have a kind of pride, I guess, about things like that. I don't like to take a girl out in her father's car. If I can't take her in my own, then, by golly, we'll walk."

Mr. Chelton nodded approvingly. "I used to feel the same way, Andy."

"Andy," Betty said. "Come here a minute and tell me what to do. If I move this way, and this, and this, I might get to the king row, but I'm afraid."

Andy looked over her shoulder. "You're right to be afraid. Your worthy opponent would slaughter you! You have got a move, though."

"What?"

"Uh-uh. *You* figure it."

Betty studied the board. She moved a checker but kept her fingers on it. "This?"

"Try it."

Betty removed her fingers· and her father promptly jumped his red checker over a black one.

"Gosh!" Andy said. "I never saw that one. I'm sorry, Betty. What can I do to make up?"

Betty considered. "You might take me to the Harvest Ball."

Andy was grave. "I'd love to. But I've already got a date with your sister."

"You could ditch her, couldn't you?"

"I could, but you really wouldn't want me to do that, would you?"

"Yes, I would. She'd let you ditch me, if it were the other way around, I bet."

Andy grinned. "Think so? Don't you know that if I had a date with you, she couldn't keep me from it?"

"Honest? Cross your heart?"

"Cross my heart." Andy did so.

"Then," Betty said, "the very first time I go to a Harvest Ball I'm going with you."

"Good. How long will I have to wait? Four years? Five?"

"Two. *I*," Betty said grandly, "intend to go when I'm eleven!"

Jean had listened with amusement and a warm affection for both of them. In some ways, she thought, he's nicer to her than Bill. What a darling he is! She said, as they walked across town, "I hope Betty didn't embarrass you."

"Betty? Gosh, no. I like her. She's quite a girl. Not the girl her sister is, you understand, but give her a few years—"

"Two," Jean interposed.

He chuckled. "That's right, two. Honestly, she looked so serious and sounded so cute, darned if I wasn't tempted

116

to do as she suggested and ditch you."

"Just try it."

"I know better. Listen, are you warm enough? This wind is really something."

"I'm fine." She was. The wind, bitter though it might be, could not affect her.

"We'd better walk a little faster. What do you bet the snow comes tonight?"

"I'll bet what you bet."

He laughed. "No mind of your own. Well, I just hope we get it before Thanksgiving. Mom asked me today if I'd like to have you come for Thanksgiving dinner."

"She did?" The idea surprised her. She had never thought of having Thanksgiving dinner anywhere but home. Still, to go to Andy's—what fun that would be!

"Yep. How about it? Will you come?"

"I'd love to. I don't know what my family will think, but I know what *I* think."

"Good." He took her arm. "Mom's anxious to meet you."

"I'm anxious to meet her. I was beginning to wonder if I ever would."

"You were beginning to wonder—Chelton, for gosh sakes! Have you been thinking I didn't *want* you two to meet?"

"No. That is, well—sort of."

"Jean, I never thought. Gosh, I don't know what to say." He bent his head against the wind and scuffed his heels. Suddenly he stopped. "I know! Why don't we go and see her now?"

"Tonight? But I—are you sure she wouldn't mind?"

"She'd love it." He grabbed her hand. "Come on!"

She held back. "Do I look all right?"

"You look half-frozen."

"I mean, am I dressed all right?"

He laughed at her. "What's the matter? Think you ought to go home and change to a formal?"

"Andy, you're no help."

He relented. "You look fine. Mom will be crazy about you. Move, Chelton, before our blood congeals."

CHAPTER EIGHTEEN

Andy lived in the second floor apartment of a converted one family house. As they climbed the stairs of the outside entrance he said, "I don't see any lights. Mom must be in the kitchen. Or maybe she's lying down."

Jean was nervous. "Andy, are you sure she won't mind? We could come some other time, when she's expecting us."

He was preceding her up the stairs so that he could show her the way. "I'm sure. Gosh, I'm glad the Menningers have all their lights on. Of course, I could do these stairs with my eyes shut, but you—"

The Menningers were the people who lived on the first floor and, as they'd approached the house, Jean had seen the father and mother and three pajama-clad children through the window.

"Here we are," Andy said. "Wait a minute, while I get the key." He lifted a key from under the rubber door mat. "We always keep it locked on account of Mom being alone so much."

He opened the door into darkness. "Mom?"

There was no answer.

"Mom?" he called in a louder voice.

Still no response.

"That's funny," he said, and flicked a light switch just inside the door. "Come in, Jean, while I have a look."

Jean stepped into a small, square entrance way, from which a long hall ran toward the back of the house. Five doors opened from the hall and, as Andy disappeared through the one farthest from them, she looked around with interest. All of these rooms, she thought, must once have been bedrooms. Probably two of them still are. Which would leave a kitchen, a bathroom and a living room. Yes, that would be about right.

She felt a sudden excitement. This was where Andy

lived. This was where he studied, and ate, and worked, and slept, and listened to records, and talked to her on the phone. Where was the phone? Right here, in this entrance, on a small table against the wall and oh, joy, there was a mirror above it! She could fix her hair before Andy's mother saw her.

There wasn't time. Andy was back. He had a sheet of white paper in his hand. "She isn't here. Look, she left me a note." He extended the paper to Jean.

Jean didn't take it. "She isn't here? But I thought—where is she?"

"She's gone to spend the night with the Webster children. Mrs. Webster is a friend of hers at the office. The note says she was rushed to the hospital for an emergency appendectomy. Her husband called Mom. Here, read it for yourself." Again he held out the paper and this time Jean took it.

She read slowly. She'd been apprehensive about meeting Andy's mother, but filled with excitement at the prospect. Now that the meeting was not to take place she felt cheated. "I guess that takes care of that."

Andy was apparently feeling much as she did. "A good idea while it lasted, but it certainly didn't last very long. What do we do now? Head for the Y?"

"I suppose." The prospect wasn't appealing. She realized that, in addition to meeting his mother, she'd been wanting to see Andy in his home setting. Now she was to be denied even that. She hesitated. "Before we go, tell me, which is your room?"

He gestured toward one of the closed doors. "That one. Want to see it?"

"No." She did want to see it, but the thought suggested an intimacy for which she wasn't prepared. Had his mother been here it might have been different.

He continued explaining. "That's the kitchen back there, and the bath. Mom's room is up here, across from the living room. Speaking of living, why don't you come in and get warm before we start out again?"

She was, she thought hysterically, already in. But she would decline the invitation. It wouldn't be right. Not when there was no one else here. "Andy, I don't think—"

He sensed her reluctance. "Listen, if you're worried

119

about chaperones, we've got the whole Menninger clan downstairs. And we won't stay any longer than a few minutes."

Well, of course! The Menningers did make a difference. "All right. But just for a few minutes."

He preceded her into the living room, turned on two lamps, and grinned. "Come into my parlor."

She giggled. "Hello, spider."

"Hello, fly."

He waved an arm. "Home sweet home. What do you think of it?"

The room was small and showed no particular imagination in its furnishings, but it looked comfortable and lived in. There were an overstuffed sofa and chair slip-covered in striped denim. There was a gatelegged table with the side pieces dropped, and it had two chairs. There was a bookcase, two occasional tables, a television set and three lamps. The flowered paper on the walls looked more suitable for a bedroom than for a living room. The blue rug was the usual nine-by-twelve size and a good two feet of wooden floor bordered it on three sides. The sofa covered most of the exposed part on the fourth.

"It's darling," Jean said. "I love that table by the window. Is that where you eat your meals?"

"Only when we have company. Most of the time we eat in the kitchen. But on Thanksgiving, when you're here, we'll struggle with the extension piece, and table pads, and all that stuff. You'll see."

"I can hardly wait."

"Neither can I."

She walked to the bookcase and picked up a framed photograph of a rather young looking man. "Your father?"

He came to stand beside her. "Yes. Not a bad looking guy, huh?"

"He's—he was very nice looking. You resemble him a little, Andy."

"An outright flatterer, that's you, Chelton."

"No. I mean it. I wish I could have known him."

"So do I."

She replaced the picture. "Are these your books?"

"Some of them. Hey, if you're going to start reading,

120

don't you think you'd better take off your jacket?"

She had knelt by the bookcase, but now she looked up at him, confused. "Why, we both have our jackets on!"

"I know. We'd better get out of them. If we don't we'll perish the minute we stick our noses outside."

"I guess you're right." She slipped out of her jacket and handed it to him, then went back to the books, withdrew a small, worn volume entitled *Little Masterpieces,* and flipped its pages. " 'The Fall of the House of Usher,' " she read. " 'Ligeia,' but I'm probably not pronouncing it right."

Andy had laid their jackets across the back of the large chair. "You're not. This 'Ligeia' that you can't pronounce was Poe's favorite story."

"How do you know?"

"I know everything about that guy. He fascinates me. He was born before his time, though. He'd have been a natural today."

"Which one of his stories do you like best?"

" 'MS. Found in a Bottle,' I think. Boy, what an imagination!"

She sat back on the floor. "Andy, I believe you mean it. You really go for this stuff."

"Sure, I do. Oh, I know I'm a square, but if you could read it the way I do I bet you'd like it, too."

"I've tried reading it, but I never understood it. Andy, listen—" She'd had a sudden idea, and it filled her with inner excitement. "Why don't you read one of his stories to me?"

He stared. "Now?"

"Yes!"

"But what about—we were only going to stay here a few minutes. What about the dance?"

"Oh, let's forget the dance."

His expression was odd. "But I thought you were afraid—I mean, I wouldn't want to stay if you thought—"

It was funny, she thought, that only a short time before she had decided that it wouldn't be right to linger. And now Andy was showing unwillingness. Somehow, his very unwillingness was reassuring. "Stop worrying. You said yourself that the Menningers would take care of the proprieties. I get so tired of going to the record hops all the time. And there couldn't be anything more harmless than reading Poe, could there?"

He grinned. "No. But nobody'd believe that's what we were doing."

"The heck with what people believe! Please, Andy!"

"Well, if you're sure—"

"Of course, I'm sure. I'm going to sit right over there at one end of the sofa, and you sit at the other end, under the lamp, where I can watch you."

Andy followed instructions. He opened the book and cleared his throat. "Well, there's a quotation here at the beginning, and I don't know what it means. I guess it's French. Anyway, this is the way the story begins." He cleared his throat again, glanced at her, and made a wry face. "Talk about your square situations.—this is the square root of the square."

Jean smiled. "An interesting beginning. What's the story about? Mathematics?"

"Shut up, Chelton. Another crack like that and there will be no story. I don't know yet why I'm doing this."

"I do."

"Why?"

"Because I asked you to."

"Yeah. And, obviously, I'm your slave. Well, here goes again. *Of my country and of my family I have little to say. Ill usage and length of years have driven me from the one, and estranged me from the other. Hereditary wealth afforded me an education of no common order, and a contemplative turn of mind enabled me to—* Jean, this is—screwy. I can't read it so it sounds right."

"Well, tell me about it then, I'm curious."

"Really? Okay. There was this guy, see, who went off on a ship with a bunch of other guys, and they were anchored along the coast of Java when a storm came up. It was a real scientific phenomenon, this storm, and it hit the ship, and everyone was killed except this guy and an old Swede. Look, how can I tell you a story when you're sitting way over there and I'm way over here?"

"You could come closer."

"I will." He did so promptly and put his arm around her. "Lean back, Angel, get comfortable. This is a long story. And so," he went on, "they floated around, this guy

122

and the Swede, for five days, and the sixth day never came."

"They died," Jean said, "thereby ending the story."

He turned her face toward his and touched her nose reprovingly. "They did no such thing. Do you want to know what happened, or don't you?"

"I want to know."

"All right, then. Let's have no more of this heckling. When the sun went down, all the fire went out of it. It became only a rim, and it went into the ocean, and everything got queer."

"Including the Swede?"

"In one minute, now, I'm going to spank you. Whose story is this, anyway? What was queer was that there was no more light at all. They were still in the ocean, but they'd sailed beyond the point of light, I guess, and they were surrounded by darkness, and they kept going up in the air because of these high waves, and then they'd sink down into the bottom of the waves. Everything was black and it was pretty awful."

"I should imagine."

"Nothing like what came later, though. Because when they were clear down at the bottom of one of these black pits they looked up and there, towering over them, was another ship, a crazy souped-up looking one."

"How could they see it, if it was so dark?"

"I don't know. They just could. Anyway, they knew the ship was coming down on top of them, and it did. The Swede got killed and this guy got tossed right up on the other ship and everything *there* was pretty queer, too."

"Naturally."

"Enough, Chelton. What it all boils down to is that this guy begins to write down everything that happens, with the idea that he'll put his manuscript in a bottle. It's gruesome, because what they're actually doing is whirling around on the brink of eternity."

"I don't get it."

He sighed. "I didn't think you would."

"Well, go on. What's the rest?"

"That's about it. She plunges over. The ship, I mean."

"And that's *all?*"

"Yep."

"But that's crazy!"

"Sure. That's what makes it so interesting."

"For you, maybe. You've got a scientific mind. Me, I'm getting sleepy." She pulled away from him, stretched her arms high, and yawned.

"A fine thing," Andy said. "After all the trouble I've gone to, you yawn in my face."

"It's just that I'm so comfortable. I don't understnad the story, but I loved the way you told it, Andy."

"I'll tell you another some day."

"All right." She slumped and leaned against him. "I suppose we ought to go, but I hate to move."

"Me, too."

They sat in silence for several minutes. Then Andy said, "Jean, I've been thinking. I guess it's what I said about telling you another story some day that got me started. After we're married, when we have a place of our own, we'll have a lot of nights like this. Nights when it's cold, and we won't be going anywhere."

"I know," Jean said softly. A sudden shyness kept her from adding that she'd been thinking the same thing.

"We won't want to go anywhere because it will be enough just to be together."

"Is that the way you feel, Andy? Truly?"

Andy looked straight into her eyes. "It's the way I feel. As far as I'm concerned, Jean, there will never be enough time for just being together. I want to spend all my time with you, and not break up for hours the way we have to do now. I want you in our own home, cooking my meals, and loving me, and—and—" He turned her in his arms so that she was facing him. "Jean, I wish we were married right now. This very minute!"

"I wish we were, too." She felt a great tenderness toward him. To be here, in his home, listening to him, watching the expression on his face, loving him—what more could there be, except—well, except being married, and having all this forever?

"Jean," he said. "Jean, I—" His eyes glowed as he bent his head, and just before his lips touched hers, she thought: Why, that's funny! There's no longer any green in his eyes! Right now they're all brown!

She closed her own eyes, then, and kissed him back.

124

"Andy," she whispered. "Oh, Andy."

It was probably a half hour later when Jean became conscious of a vague disquiet in the back of her mind. At first it was nothing tangible, but gradually the sense of uneasiness increased until she recognized it for what it was. She and Andy were no longer sitting, but were *lying* on the sofa. For an instant the thought startled her so much that she almost got up. But then Andy kissed her again and it was such a sweet kiss and she liked it so much that she didn't move.

Her uneasiness subsided. She felt so happy and so loved and so loving. She felt as though she and Andy were in a very special world of their own. It was like being on that ship he'd told her about. They were whirling and whirling. Just the two of them. On the brink of eternity . . .

The crash came from downstairs and its effect was so shocking that for a stunned moment Jean thought: We've plunged over! The ship is carrying us down! Then she heard a child's scream, running footsteps, and a woman's reassuring voice. She became rigid. She wasn't in a ship. She was in Andy Decker's apartment. She was alone with him in his apartment and, downstairs, one of the Menninger children had fallen out of bed!

Dazed, she sat up. "Andy," she said. "Andy, what's happened to us? Do you realize that we almost—?" She began to cry.

Andy, too, sat up and looked at her. He started to put an arm around her, but she shuddered and moved beyond reach. "Don't cry, Jean. Oh, gosh, please don't. Listen. We *didn't,* you know."

"We could have," Jean sobbed. "Andy, if that child downstairs hadn't fallen—Andy, I can't stand the way I feel. I mean, we came so close, and I never intended—I never thought I could be so—"

"Jean, stop it." His hair was rumpled, and his shirt. "Angel, I'm sorry. Please believe that I'm sorry. I didn't intend to go so far, either. I guess I just got carried away. And I—darn it, Jean, I told you, once, that I was no boy. I mean, gosh! When a girl kisses back the way you did, what's a guy supposed to think? Besides, I happen to love you. Had you forgotten that?"

"Love?" Jean said. "You call that love? That—that—"

She couldn't find a description. "If you really loved me you would never have allowed yourself to *get* so carried away!"

Andy began to look less abject. His face hardened. "Well, that's really good, Chelton. It wasn't *all* my fault, you know. And sure, maybe we gave in to natural impulses a little, but we stopped, didn't we?"

"Yes, we stopped. But only because of what happened downstairs. Why don't you admit it, Andy? You didn't *want* to stop, did you?"

"No, darn it, I didn't." He spoke defiantly. "Right now I feel as though somebody had hit me with a sledge."

"You're just trying to get my sympathy. But it won't work. I think we were being just awful, and I—"

"You mean you didn't like it?"

"That's just it! I *did!* But I don't think I should, and I'm so mixed up I don't know what's right, or what's wrong, or—or anything. Andy, I think you'd better take me home."

Andy looked at her for a whole minute, and then he got to his feet. "I'll get your jacket."

In silence they put on their wraps. Andy turned off the lamps and they walked toward the outside door. "Jean, I—"

"Please don't say anything. Not now. Just take me home."

The stairs creaked as they walked down. The cold struck them with the impact of a physical slap. The wind howled derisively. In the Menninger apartment everything was quiet once again.

CHAPTER NINETEEN

Toward morning Jean fell asleep. All night long she had asked herself questions. But she had found no answers. The questions had gone on and on, endlessly.

It was eleven o'clock when Betty called her to the

phone. Jean sat up in bed, sensing, in a vague way, that something was wrong. Consciousness, when it came, was a dull ache. Last night she and Andy—Andy! She ran for the stairs. The call must be from him.

"Jean," he said. "I ducked out for a few minutes. I had to call you. You wouldn't say anything last night, and you wouldn't let me say anything, and I've been nearly crazy, wondering. Jean, what are you thinking?"

"I'm not sure what I'm thinking. I can't seem to straighten things out in my mind."

"You do know that I'm sorry?"

"Yes, I know that. I'm sorry, too. I wish it weren't necessary for either of us to .be sorry, though."

"So do I." He sounded abject. "Jean, last night, when I left you, you acted as though you didn't even want to see me again. But we've got to talk. We've just got to. You realize that, don't you?"

"I suppose so."

"You suppose? Jean, it's an absolute necessity! We can't leave things just dangling. We've got to decide where we are and where we're heading. I'm coming for you tonight, and we'll go—I don't know—somewhere. I'll be there at eight."

"All right." She hung up the receiver. She thought: What I told him is true. I can't seem to get things straightened out. But I've got nine hours in which to make up my mind as to what, exactly, I do think.

The nine hours dragged. Betty told her, once, that she looked awful, and her mother asked her, late in the afternoon, if she were moping about anything. Nothing they said had any real effect on her. She was immersed in her own problem and, as the day went on, she discovered that her conclusions, such as they were, were anything but happy.

Andy arrived promptly. The Ramshack, he said, was fixed, and was she ready to leave?

Mrs. Chelton asked where they were going and Andy looked to Jean for the answer.

"To the dance, probably," she said.

But they didn't go to the dance. They didn't go to Grandy's, or to Miller's, or any place where they might be interrupted by friends. They went to a small restaurant on

127

the other side of town, a restaurant to which neither of them had ever been. Their choice was a good one for the isolation they wanted. It was past the hour for dinner patrons and too early for the after movie crowd.

They sat in a corner booth and the waitress brought glasses of water and menus. "Dinner?" she asked. "I c'n recommend the roast beef. The veal cutlet's all gone."

"No dinners," Andy said. "We'll have two hamburgs, a plate of French fries, and two root beers."

The waitress scribbled on her pad. "Large or small root beers?"

"Large." He said to Jean, when the girl had gone, "I suppose you're not hungry, either, but we can't sit here without ordering. If it weren't so cold, we could park somewhere, but as it is—" He shrugged.

"I know." Jean unfolded a paper napkin and placed it in her lap. She felt strangely embarrassed. She had known that she must talk with Andy, and yet, now that the opportunity was here, it seemed such a public place to discuss anything other than very general topics. She read the juke box selections from the coin machine on the wall at her left, then reread them.

"Want some music?" Andy asked.

"No thanks."

He seemed as hesitant about talking as she. He didn't look at her but studied the sign on the opposite wall that read: TRY OUR SUBMARINE SANDWICH. She had drunk all the water in her glass before he finally turned his gaze toward her. When he spoke his words were impersonal. "Quite a snow we had today. It must have started early."

She said, before she thought, "It started about two o'clock this morning. That is—"

He leaned forward slightly. "Didn't you sleep, either?"

He'd used the word *either*. That meant that he, too, had been awake. "No," she said. "I couldn't sleep. Not after—"

"That makes two of us." He sighed. "You know, all day, I've been thinking of what I was going to say to you, and now I can't seem to remember any of it."

She lifted her water glass, saw that it was empty, and put it down. "I wish *I* knew what to say. All I can do is

128

try. Andy, listen. I used to think I knew all the answers. I mean, I'd read all the books I was supposed to, and even some I wasn't supposed to, and I'd had courses in physiology and biology and I'd been taught to believe in the Ten Commandments. And so I figured that I was—immune, I guess. I thought that only girls like—well, like that Rosalie, would allow boys to make love to them in the way you made love to me last night. The one exception was Gee. And even with Gee, I figured that she'd been driven to it. But now I find that I'm no different from anyone else. So what does that make of me?"

"Jean, stop." Andy's voice was ragged. "Don't ever compare yourself with Rosalie. Or Gee. You're talking as though we'd gone all the way."

"That's just it," Jean said dully. "We would have, if it hadn't been for the Menninger child. We were past the point of knowing, or caring, I'm sure we were. And that's what frightens me. Because I know, now, that there is no such thing as immunity. It could happen to anyone."

"Jean, please. You're being too rough on yourself. Last night was my fault. All of it."

"Andy, you didn't plan it?"

"No, I didn't plan it. But I know the danger signals. And you don't."

"What do you mean?"

"Listen. Do you remember, last week, after we'd had a fight, how we sat in front of your house and how we necked for a while?"

"Yes."

"Do you also remember how I shoved you out of the car and into the house?"

"Yes, I do. I wondered why."

"That's what I thought. You didn't know, then. But you ought to, now."

She stared at him. "So *that's* the reason—but I never realized— Oh! That must be why, last night, you didn't want to—" She stopped at his warning "Sh!"

The waitress deposited plates and glasses on the table. A little root beer sloshed over one of the glasses and she wiped it with a damp rag. "Catsup?" she asked. "Mustard?"

"Neither. This is fine, thank you," Andy said, and she went away again.

Now Jean stared at the bun and at the two crisp pickle chips which lay beside it. She made no move to eat.

"Andy," she said finally. "Last night you didn't want to stay in the apartment. Was it because you were afraid of what might happen?"

"What do *you* think?"

"I believe you were. But Andy, if you knew, then—" She stopped, conscious of a dull, dragging weariness. With effort she roused herself to the point of saying what had to be said. "Then I'm not the first girl with whom you ever—" Again she stopped.

"I'm no kid."

"I'm beginning to understand that." The words had a wooden sound for, in a moment of painful comprehension, she had remembered what Bill had told her. Georgia, Georgia and Andy and Breck Hill.

She sat erect. There was no weariness within her now. "I'm beginning to understand a lot of things. You've made a point of telling me, several times, that you were no boy. You stopped being a boy when you went with Georgia Kane, didn't you?"

His eyes were shocked. "Georgia? What has Georgia got to do with this? Or with us?"

"Plenty. You went with her for two years. And maybe you think I'm too dumb to know this, but Georgia has the reputation for being—well, for being the way boys want her. So don't think you can sit there and act so darned innocent about her!"

"I'm not trying to act innocent about her," Andy said. "You're the one who mentioned her."

"Why shouldn't I? You didn't, and somebody ought to, under the circumstances."

"What circumstances?" He was making a show of bewilderment. Show only, she decided. He knew perfectly well.

"Must I draw a map? Don't think I don't know what went on between you two because I do! But that doesn't mean I have to like it. That doesn't mean that I have to take what's left after she's through with you! That doesn't mean—"

130

Andy's face became white. "Stop it, Jean. You've got no right to say those things."

"Haven't I?" Her voice became higher. "That's right, I haven't! Oh, I did have, once. Once, I was a fool. Once, I believed a boy who said he loved me. Once, I wore his ring. No more!" She pulled the ring from her finger and threw it on the table. "We're through, Andy Decker! I don't intend to be another Georgia Kane! You can go back to the first one, and I hope you'll be happy!"

Andy looked at the ring, then at her, and she was startled by what she saw in his face. If anything, his anger exceeded her own. But all he said was, "All right, Chelton. If that's the way you want it."

Jean grabbed her jacket from the rack beside their booth. "That's the way I want it."

She left him sitting there, still staring at the ring and at the untouched food. Let him, she thought vindictively, make his own explanations to the waitress as to why she had gone.

CHAPTER TWENTY

Most difficult, for Jean, was the adjustment. She'd worn Andy's ring. She'd gone steady. Now she was doing neither. Now there was only a smooth shiny place on her finger where the ring had been. Now there was only a boy in her home room who spoke to her when he met her face to face, but whose voice and manner were completely expressionless. Now there were questions to be answered. One question, really. Why was she no longer going with Andy? To her friends and to her family she gave the same answer. They no longer clicked, she said. They'd decided to break up. It was only when she asked herself the same question that the answer varied.

By Thanksgiving week Jean knew what pride had kept her from admitting earlier. She still loved Andy. If he were to ask her, she'd go out with him again. If he were to ask her, she'd wear his ring. If he were to ask her, she'd go anywhere with him, anywhere in the world. If he were to ask her . . .

He didn't ask her. To go out, or to wear his ring, or to go anywhere in the world. He did something that plunged her more deeply than ever into wretchedness. He took Georgia Kane to the Harvest Ball.

Typically, it was Liz who called, on Thanksgiving morning, to pass along this bit of news. Virginia had called, too, but she hadn't mentioned it. She'd had, Jean thought, more tact. Liz said, "I hate to tell you, but I thought you ought to know."

"Why?" Jean asked. She was proud of her coolness.

"Well, you'd planned to go with Andy, yourself, and I thought—"

"I'd planned to, yes. But that was while we were going together. We haven't dated for several weeks, Liz. You know that."

"Yes, but I—honestly, doesn't it bother you at all?"

"Why should it?"

Liz sounded huffy. "I must say you're awfully *calm*. What I wanted to tell you was that I didn't think Andy was having a very good time. Georgia looked stunning, though."

"Liz, I don't care whether Andy had a good time or not. As for Georgia looking stunning, she always does, so that's not news. What about you? Did you have a good time?"

"Divine."

"How did you get along with Barney?"

"Oh, *beautifully*. You know, he'd really awfully cute, Jean. He has this way of looking at you, but not looking, that's—"

She launched into a description that would go on, Jean knew, for some time. She was glad Liz couldn't see her. Liz would have loved these tears. She'd have made a big thing of being solicitous, an even bigger thing than she was making of Barney's charms.

"And so," Liz concluded, "we have a date tonight. Isn't that absolutely *marv?*"

"Absolutely," Jean said. "Have fun, and call me tomorrow."

Jean replaced the receiver and walked to the kitchen. She opened the oven door and sniffed the turkey, then asked her mother if she needed help with dinner.

"You might clean the celery," Mrs. Chelton said. "Oh, and after a while, will you check the table to see if Betty forgot anything? Maggie's coming, you know, and we want everything to be nice."

"Yes," Jean said. "Of course. We want everything to be nice. We mustn't forget that Maggie is coming, must we? We mustn't forget anything. Ever. We must always remember."

"Jean, aren't you feeling well?" Her mother's voice was concerned.

"I'm feeling fine," Jean said. "Why not? This is Thanksgiving, and it only comes once a year, and it's such a happy occasion. We sit down and we thank God for all our blessings, even if we haven't got any, and we all eat too much and then we do dishes for hours and hours. Oh, yes, and we take a nap, *if* we're lucky enough to get to sleep."

"Jean," Mrs. Chelton said. "I don't know what's bothering you, although perhaps I can guess. You aren't the first girl to quarrel with her boy friend, you know. You won't be the last. I haven't asked you about Andy because I figured you'd tell me when you were ready. But I *am* asking you to soft pedal your own unhappiness. I want you to at least make an effort. Bill's so happy that Maggie's coming, and if you do anything to spoil their day, I—" She hesitated. "I can't spank you, darling. Why don't you go for a walk? Maybe, when you come back, you'll feel better."

"All right, Mother."

She put on her wraps. The pain that had begun after Liz called was growing. She'd lost Andy to Georgia. And it was her own fault.

She walked through snow-drifted streets. Down one block, turn right, down another, turn left. Walk straight for three more. Where was she going? It didn't matter. One direction was as good as another. Forward, backward, sideward, what difference?

She was in the downtown section, walking past the Cottage Restaurant, when she heard a sound that caused

133

her to jump toward the curb. From the slanted roof of the restaurant the snow had cascaded, bringing with it the heavy icicles hanging from the eaves. She stared, in awed fascination, at the broken particles of ice, and a passer-by, a man she had never seen before, said, "That was a close one, Miss. It's a good thing you jumped."

"Yes," she said. "It was, I'd hate to think where I'd be right now if I'd jumped the other way."

She took a deep breath as the impact of her own words hit her. *If I'd jumped the other way.* Direction *did* make a difference. And people always had a choice.

Why, that was it! That was what had been troubling her most during these past weeks! But just because she'd made a mistake once she didn't have to keep *on* making it, over and over, did she? She had a choice! She could jump the other way!

She turned and retraced her steps. But now she walked quickly.

Maggie was sitting on the sofa with Bill, and, as Jean entered the living room, she said, "Hi, there, Jean. Don't tell me you've been out on a date this early in the day!"

Jean grinned. "You're out on one, aren't you? But no, I haven't. I've been walking." She looked at her mother, whose expression was questioning. "I've been working up an appetite. I'm starved."

Mrs. Chelton's face lost its concern and Jean thought: I guess I've been a problem to her as well as to myself. She remembered her mother's comment about wanting everything nice for Maggie and, hoping her mother would understand that she was trying, she said, "Maggie, you look especially super today."

Maggie did. She sparkled. She looked at Bill, Bill looked at her, and then they both nodded. "There's a reason," Maggie said. "We want you all to know. I've finally convinced this lug that he can't live without me. We plan to get married over the Christmas holiday."

It wasn't fair! Why should Maggie and Bill have what she and Andy never could? And then she thought: No. For them it's right. They've waited until they were old enough to be very sure. They can't miss!

She went to Maggie and hugged her.

DECEMBER

CHAPTER TWENTY-ONE

People had a saying they were fond of repeating at this time of the year. Winter, they said, had settled in. Farmhouse porches were drifted over with snow, as were fences. A road in Launee Park had been closed off for coasting. The skating rink was frozen over. Workers in the city street department labored nightly to clear away snow. Every day the morning paper reported accidents in which cars had skidded and gone out of control.

Housewives were busy making steamed puddings and mincemeat cookies, to be frozen and stored until Christmas. The post office was plastered with MAIL EARLY signs. Shoppers lingered in the downtown stores, fingering merchandise, consulting lists, losing wallets, opening charge accounts. School children rehearsed for Christmas plays, or Christmas song festivals, and began to talk of Christmas parties. Every club, civic or otherwise, planned a gift exchange.

This had always been the season Jean liked best. Christmas, for her, had never been limited to one day, but had been celebrated for a whole month. She'd spent hours, in the past, planning gifts for her parents, and Bill, and Betty, and Maggie, and Virginia. She'd thought, earlier, that this year she would have another name to add to her gift list. She had thought, once, that gloves would be perfect for Andy, but she couldn't give gloves to a boy she now saw only in school.

Since Thanksgiving she'd been conscious of a change in herself. For one thing, she felt older. The most marked change, though, was in her tolerance. Virginia had commented on this. "You never condemn people. Even the ones who deserve it. Why, the other day, you even defended Georgia Kane when some of the girls were talking about her."

"Oh, well," Jean had said. "Who's to say who deserves

condemnation? We're all human, I guess."

She didn't realize that it was philosophy of this sort that was helping her. She knew only that she felt better than she had for some time. She was more quiet, perhaps, but she was making a determined effort to be her best self.

Her determination was rewarded, early in December, when she received her report of the second six weeks' grades. With trepidation she slipped the card from its envelope, and glanced first at the column to the right of the subject titled Problems of Democracy. She'd made a B! She was so pleased that she made a point of stopping, after school, to tell Mr. Malon of her delight.

"You've earned it, Miss Chelton," he said in his old-fashioned way. "You are to be commended."

"I'm very happy."

"You'll be interested to know that your happiness extends to myself. It's never pleasant for a teacher to give failing, or conditional, grades."

"No, I suppose not. I'm glad you didn't have to give a second one to this particular student."

Her mother said, when she took her report home, "Congratulations, darling." Her father said, "I knew you could do it." And Betty said, "Have we got something to celebrate all of a sudden? Are we going to get ice cream or anything?"

It was gratifying, all of it, but she wished, sometimes, that her life were a little less dull. She took part in few social activities. She was seeing more of Virginia than she had in months, and she enjoyed the long talks that seemed like a reaffirmation of friendship. She saw very little of Liz, but this was only natural, for Liz was going steady again and most of her time was concentrated on Barney.

Jean didn't miss Liz. She wondered, at times, how Liz felt about Leroy, and she thought: It certainly didn't take her long to get over him. She couldn't have been as serious about him as I was, as I still am, about Andy.

When she thought of Andy now it was with regret for her own high-handed breaking off with him. She had better perspective than she'd had at the time she'd thrown his ring on the table. Then she'd been upset—shocked, really, by her first contact with human weakness, especially her own. But now that she'd had time to get some perspective, she supposed that most people came up against the same sort of thing sooner or later. Now she knew what could happen, even to nice people. It was infinitely better to know than to be protected from such knowledge.

Bill had tried to give her this protection but he'd been wrong. His motives had been typically those of a big brother. She didn't know, but she had an idea that he and Maggie, loving each other as they did, and having gone together for years, had come up against the same kind of problem. That they'd licked the problem she didn't doubt. They'd jumped the right way.

Georgia Kane hadn't. Having encountered her own weakness, she'd gone along with it. She hadn't been strong enough to resist.

All of which made *what* of Andy? The fact that Andy had gone with Georgia for so long was the one irreconcilable factor. It just didn't fit! Not with the Andy she knew. Not with the Andy her parents and Betty knew. And liked. Not with the Andy Bill would have liked had he taken the time to know him. There had to be an explanation, but what was it?

About the middle of December Miss Henderson told her English IV classes that she was giving them an assignment to be turned in on January fifth. Everyone moaned. January fifth was the day on which school would resume after the Christmas holiday. Wasn't it exactly like the old work horse?

"Some of you," she said, "have not yet learned to appreciate the richness of content to be found in our great classics. I have decided that if you were to know more about the writers, themselves, your appreciation of their writings might be deepened. I am asking each of you to choose one author from the list I am distributing. You will do a source paper on your particular author in the light of one, and one only, of his writings. Please don't forget to include a bibliography."

Jean, along with others in her class, scanned the list with resentment. Even if she started immediately she'd have to give some of her precious vacation time to a study of—which one would it be? Dickens? No, his writings were too drippy. All that Tiny Tim stuff was sickening. Thackeray? Too stodgy. Shakespeare? She'd had all she

137

wanted of Shakespeare in *Macbeth*. Who, then? She went back through the list and saw a name she'd missed on first skimming. Edgar Allan Poe. This was for her! Poe was Andy's favorite. If she studied him she would feel just a little closer to Andy. She wouldn't even wait until vacation. She would go to the public library tonight!

The library was quiet. Few people were there, and most of them were elderly. Jean walked past the rental section and went directly to the files. She noted, on a scratch pad, the catalogue numbers of available source books, then moved to the reference shelves in the rear. She found the volumes she wanted, sat down at a large table, and began to take notes.

Poe, E. A., she wrote. B. Boston, 1809, d. Baltimore, 1849, regarded by many as our greatest poet. She stopped writing. This must be the wrong Poe! The one she wanted wasn't a poet, he'd written science fiction! She'd have to check the files again. She sighed, and got to her feet, but she didn't move, because there, right behind her, was Andy Decker!

"Hello, Jean," he said. He glanced toward the front desk where Miss Ramsay, the librarian, sat, then lowered his voice. "I saw you when I came in, but you were so absorbed I didn't want to disturb you."

"Oh," she said, and her voice, too, was almost a whisper. "I didn't see you. I didn't even hear you."

"What are you doing?"

"That source thing for Miss Henderson."

"Me, too. Who'd you take?"

"Oh, I haven't really decided." She tried to stand so that her back would hide the books on the table, but he moved around her and glanced at them. "Poe," he said, and then he said it again. *"Poe!"* This time he forgot to keep his voice low and Miss Ramsay looked up from her desk and shook her head warningly.

Andy looked at her. "Jean," he whispered. "Why Poe?"

"Because—well, because I—"

"The truth, Jean. Please?"

"Well, *you* liked him, and I thought—"

"Wow!" Andy said. In the silence of the library the single word reverberated with the force of an explosion. An elderly woman three tables away dropped her newspaper and stared reprovingly. Miss Ramsay jumped to her feet and started toward them, but Andy had Jean by the hand and was meeting the librarian halfway. "Never mind, Miss Ramsay," he said. "We were just leaving."

Then they were standing outside the library, at the top of the steps. It was a beautiful night. The snow was coming down in large, soft flakes. The lights of the decorated hemlock tree in front of the building glowed red and green and blue and amber. Jean was still trying to assimilate the fact that she was here and that Andy was beside her. Things don't happen this way, she thought.

But they did. Andy looked at her. "Before we say anything, or do anything, I want to know one thing. Am I right in believing that you chose Poe for your source paper because you haven't forgotten?"

"Yes."

"Then, you—?"

She nodded.

"Okay. That's established. Where are we going, Chelton?"

"Home," she said.

They walked down the steps.

CHAPTER TWENTY-TWO

An hour later Jean and Andy were in the Chelton living room. Jean was in her father's favorite chair and Andy sat on the ottoman, with his long legs stretched toward the softly glowing fire.

Earlier, when they came in, Jean had wondered about her parents' reaction. If they were surprised, they covered up well, for they greeted Andy as though he'd been coming to the house regularly. Betty had not been so subtle. She'd said, "Why, Andy Decker! How come *you're* here? I thought you and Jean weren't going to—"

"Betty," Mrs. Chelton had interrupted. "Look what I just found! Your Christmas list!"

"I didn't know," Betty said, "that I'd lost it!"

"Maybe not, but you haven't finished it. Why don't we go upstairs and do that right now?"

"Well, all right, but I don't know why we can't stay here and finish it."

"Because," Mr. Chelton said, "I have some things to do upstairs, too, and I need your help." He winked at Andy. "Think you two can get along without us?"

So Jean's family had disappeared and, from the sound of rustling upstairs, were now engaged in wrapping packages.

Andy said, when they were gone, "They're as nice as ever. They knew, of course, that we wanted to be alone. They're giving us a chance to get things straight, aren't they?"

Andy, she thought, has never been one to lead up to things. He always plunges right in. "Yes," she said. Then she added: "Do you think we can?"

"We can try. Jean, I can't tell you how awful these past weeks have been, for me. I've felt like a heel. Oh, I admit I was pretty darned mad for a while. The last time we were together you really told me off, you know."

"I know. I'm sorry about that, Andy."

"Well, I've got a lot to be sorry for, too. I'd give anything if we could go back to the way we were before that night at my place."

"We can't go back. No one ever can. But what happened that night doesn't matter any more, Andy."

"It doesn't?" He looked at her in disbelief. "But it must! It's the reason we're no longer going steady, isn't it?"

"Not quite. Oh, maybe it's part of the reason, but not all. You see, there is also Georgia Kane."

"Yes," he said quietly, "there is also Georgia Kane. Somehow, we always come back to her, don't we? I don't know why a guy can't go with a girl, and then stop going with her, without a lot of explanations."

"Andy, I'm not asking you to explain anything."

"I know. But Georgia's been right there, between us, from the very beginning. In *your* mind, at least. I should have understood that, I guess, but I didn't. When you started yelling about her, that night in the restaurant, I couldn't believe I was hearing right. And afterward, I was so darned mad that I wanted to hurt you as much as you'd hurt me. That's why I took Georgia to the Harvest Ball." He sighed. "It was a stupid thing to do. I had a lousy time and I haven't seen her since. I hope I never see her again."

He looked at Jean. "But that isn't all you want to know, is it? I gather, from what you said in the restaurant, and from what you said a minute ago, that you read a lot more into Georgia's and my relationship than there actually was. I've thought about it a lot, since we broke up, and that's what hurt me most—the idea that you couldn't accept me as I was. I mean, I was always honest with you. I never did love anyone but you and I told you so. But, apparently, you didn't believe me. You must have had a bunch of mental reservations, right along."

"But you went with her for two years," Jean pointed out. "That's a long time to go with a girl if she doesn't mean anything to you."

"You're right about that," Andy said. "It was two years too long. Well, one, anyway. I don't know—" He rubbed his forehead. "About Georgia. Let me see if I can tell you how it was."

"Not if you don't want to, Andy." She found, to her surprise, that she meant it. "I think I've already hurt you enough."

"I do want to. I want to set the record straight, once and for all, and then forget it. Georgia was the first girl I ever went with and she was a year older than I. Do you realize what that does to a boy's ego? I was only a sophomore and here was a junior girl who'd always dated older boys, asking me to go out! I could hardly believe it, at first, but I convinced myself, in no time at all, that I was a real big shot. You should have heard me brag!"

Andy got up and poked the fire, then stood with his back to it, looking down at her. "I was the all-time dope. I thought, all the time, that she had succumbed to my fatal charm, and it never occurred to me that she was using me because she'd gone through a succession of boys and there was no one else left! By the time I wised up we were going steady, and I was too darned dumb to know how to get out of it. I tried, but she wasn't ready to let me go. Not until she had another guy lined up to take over. And I had this crazy feeling of loyalty. You see, Jean—"

He hesitated, and Jean said quickly, "Don't tell me any more." She added softly, "I think I already know." Breck Hill, she thought. Breck Hill, and a girl who had been around, and a boy who hadn't known the score. She felt a strange, mature sadness for the boy who had been so young.

"No," Andy said. "I don't think you do. In those two years with Georgia I learned a lot, but I never learned—that. I was flattered, but I never liked her enough." He was silent for a minute and then he said, "The whole, crazy, goofed up trouble is that I did like you well enough. I loved you, and I still do, which leaves me—where? Jean, what is the answer? What's to become of us?"

She thought: Isn't it strange that I, and not Andy, should be the one to know? Of course, he's never been taught, as I have, to sit on a log. "Andy," she said, "bring that ottoman over here and sit down."

He attempted a grin. "Why? Are you going to ask me for a story?"

"No, I'm going to tell you one."

And she did. She told him the story of Andy Decker and Jean Chelton, a boy and a girl who had been too young to go steady. But she didn't end it. Not quite. For how could she finish a story whose ending depended on the waiting period which lay ahead?

ABOUT THE AUTHOR

Margaret Maze Craig was born in Pennsylvania and was graduated from the Indiana State College there. During World War II, while her husband was overseas, she began to experiment with writing. First she tried greeting card verses and then she turned to articles for women's magazines. Her first full-length short story was published in *Woman's Day* and led to a request for a novel. The novel, *Trish,* was half written when the Craigs' second daughter was born.

There have been four novels since—*Julie, Marsha, Three Who Met,* and *Now that I'm Sixteen*—all enthusiastically received. Now that her two daughters are in school, Mrs. Craig has returned to teaching home economics. Her enthusiasm for her work and her concern for the problems her students face at school and at home have led to *It Could Happen to Anyone.*

Mrs. Craig lives in Oil City, Pennsylvania, and describes herself as a person with never enough time. Her interests, other than homemaking, writing, and teaching, extend to the outdoors. She is a confirmed camper and an ardent fisherwoman. She enjoys baseball and waited thirteen years for her favorite team, the Pittsburgh Pirates, to become champions.

MORE BERKLEY HIGHLAND BOOKS
THAT YOU WILL ENJOY

RADIGAN CARES   (X2093—60¢)
   by Jeannette Eyerly

AN END OF INNOCENCE   (X2161—60¢)
   by Donald Honig

MRS. MIKE   (S1590—75¢)
   by Benedict & Nancy Freedman

DROP-OUT   (X1792—60¢)
   by Jeannette Eyerly

THE BOY NEXT DOOR   (X2196—60¢)
   by Betty Cavanna

MARY ELLIS, STUDENT NURSE   (X2217—60¢)
   by Hope Newell

A LONG RIDE ON A CYCLE   (X2129—60¢)
   by James McM. Douglas

Stnd for a *free* list of all our books in print

_____

These books are available at your local newsstand, or send
price indicated plus 15¢ per copy to cover mailing costs
to Berkley Publishing Corporation, 200 Madison Avenue,
New York, N.Y. 10016.